CU00829257

A TALE FOR A LONG WINTER'S NIGHT

LORI BEASLEY BRADLEY

Copyright (C) 2017 Lori Beasley Bradley

Layout design and Copyright (C) 2020 by Next Chapter

Published 2020 by Shadow City – A Next Chapter Imprint

Edited by Lorna Read

Cover art by CoverMint

This book is a work of fiction. Names, characters, places, and incidents are the product of the author's imagination or are used fictitiously. Any resemblance to actual events, locales, or persons, living or dead, is purely coincidental.

All rights reserved. No part of this book may be reproduced or transmitted in any form or by any means, electronic or mechanical, including photocopying, recording, or by any information storage and retrieval system, without the author's permission.

What an absolutely beautiful day to be outside. It's heavenly and so much better than being cooped up in the cabin with a basket of mending.

A few white clouds drifted across the brilliant blue sky as Daisy picked her way through the patch of plump blackberries she'd found on Mill Road. She'd been checking their progress weekly and had finally decided they were ready to harvest. She'd sampled a few, and they were juicy and sweet.

I can't wait to make Papa a cobbler with these. If I get the bucket full, I should be able to put up a few pints of jam as well. Mama will like that.

The sun burned the top of her head as she scanned the small patch, and Daisy frowned. Her bucket was only half full. She pulled her skirt from the snagging thorns and inched her way back to the road. She would have to walk another half mile up the road to the next patch.

Daisy swung the wooden bucket at her side as she strolled, enjoying the soft breeze in her hair. She used her free hand to lift her thick curls so the breeze could cool her sweaty neck. The day had turned out warmer than expected.

Daisy didn't pay much heed to the approaching horses until they boxed her in near the bridge over the creek.

"Well, ain't you a pretty little thing?" the young man on a lathered roan said as he leered down at her and licked his full lips.

And aren't you rude?

Suddenly uncomfortable, Daisy turned to see another young man on a large black horse behind her. She didn't recognize the grinning blond on the horse behind her, but the man with unruly brown curls on the big roan appeared familiar.

"We seem to be lost," the curly-headed young man said, with a grin Daisy didn't trust. "Can you point us back into Paradise?"

Okay, just a couple of lost cowboys.

Daisy took a relieved breath and smiled. "You're only a couple of miles out," she said. "You go back the way you came and turn off at the first trail on your left until you come to the big creek, and then…"

The rider of the roan pushed the horse a few steps closer. "Would you mind drawin' it out for us in the dust?" he asked. "Just set your bucket down and scratch it out for us, if ya would."

What kind of cowboy can't understand simple directions?

Rolling her eyes, Daisy lowered her bucket to the road, knelt, and began scratching directions into the dust at her feet. She used her finger to make straight lines representing the roads and wavy ones to represent the streams and creeks they'd need to cross.

"Once you cross Butte Creek here," she said and stood, dusting her hand on her skirt, "it's only about a quarter-mile until you see the town."

Both riders had come closer to study her directions. When she glanced up, both men pressed close to her, and the heat from their panting mounts radiated onto her, causing her to become uneasy.

"Well, that's right nice of ya," the blond said, with a broad smile that took Daisy's eyes away from the other grinning rider.

She yelped in surprise when he reached down, grabbed her wrist, and yanked her up into his saddle.

"Come on, sweetheart," he said, as he pinned her in front of him with one strong arm. "I bet you'd like to keep company with Jake and me for a bit." He spurred his horse, and it galloped up the road with Daisy squirming and struggling.

"Let me go!" Daisy yelled and dug her nails into his hand on her bosom.

"What's she got under that skirt?" the other rider called, as he galloped beside them, laughing at Daisy struggling in front of the other rider.

He released Daisy's bosom and began yanking her skirt up to expose her bare, kicking legs. "What ya think, Jake? They shapely?"

"I think they're gonna look right nice wrapped around my waist while I'm pokin' my cock in her juicy cunny," Jake called, as they turned the horses west and headed toward the mountains.

Oh, dear lord. This isn't gonna be good for me.

"You had a cock in this cunny yet, sweetheart?" the man holding Daisy said into her ear, as his free hand reached between her sweaty thighs and grabbed a handful of pubic hair. Nobody had ever put a hand down there before, and Daisy feared what might be coming.

"Let me go!" Daisy yelled again, struggling in his arms. "You've got no right to treat me like this."

He jammed a finger into her cunny and smiled down into her horrified face. "I'm Jamison Earl, and I've got every right, sweetheart. Me and my daddy buy dirty little farm gals like you every day. When me and Jake are done with ya," he sneered, "your daddy can complain to mine, and he'll pay what ya were worth for a few pokes and some sucks."

Jamison Earl. It would figure. She'd heard about him, and none of it was good.

Jake reached over and began stroking Daisy's flailing legs. "That thing feel like it's been used before?" he asked, staring at Jamison's finger as it worked inside her.

Jamison slowed his horse, pulled his hand from between Daisy's thighs, and put the wet finger to his nose. "Smells fresh to me," he said and then stuck it in his mouth. "Tastes fresh, too."

He's as disgusting as I heard he was.

"Damn," Jake yelled and reached across to shove his hand where Jamison's had been. "My cock is hard now. Can't we just throw her down here in the weeds and get us a taste?"

Jamison spurred his horse and wrenched Jake's hand away from the girl's warm, wet cunny as the roan began moving again. "It'll be better up at the line shack," Jamison said. "I'd rather poke her on a mattress like a man than in the weeds like a damned animal."

3

"You *are* an animal!" Daisy screamed. "You're both animals."

I can't believe this is happening. What did I do? Mama's gonna say I asked for this to happen.

"And we're both gonna give it to ya like animals," Jamison said and winked at Jake as the horses labored up the trail in the afternoon heat. "We're gonna give it to ya in every hole ya got, sweetheart, and you're gonna like it so much you'll be beggin' for it every day."

What is he talking about?

That night, Daisy wept alone in the silence of the dark shack. Her body ached from the abuse it had suffered at the hands of the two young men. Her face throbbed from being slapped and punched. She tasted blood from a loosened tooth in her jaw, and it throbbed with pain.

I'm gonna be black and blue tomorrow with all the bites on my bosoms and between my legs. I can't believe they did those things to me. Do all men take their pleasure with women like that? Mama never said it would be like that.

Pain lanced up her arms from being tied to the posts above her head, and the rough rope bit into her ankles. Daisy didn't think she'd be able to sleep and flinched with every noise outside the shack. She feared they'd return to abuse her again after they finished at the saloon in town. Jamison had even threatened to bring back more of his friends.

"How many of us do you think you can take, sweetheart?" he'd jeered as he poked her cunny while Jake rammed his cock between her lips. "We have lots of friends back on the ranch who'd like a little of this."

He can't be serious.

"Let's keep this for ourselves for a while, Jamison," Jake moaned as he shoved into her mouth and released a stream of hot, bitter seed. "I don't wanna share it with them, other fellas, just yet." He rolled off her. "This is just too damned good to share yet. Let's wait 'til her holes are all stretched out from our use of 'em," he said, giggling.

Jamison chuckled and slapped Daisy's bare behind. "When we're done with ya, sweetheart, ya can rent a room upstairs at the Pair O' Dice and get a dollar a poke." He laughed. "We won't even charge ya a cut for trainin' ya up the way we are."

Tears ran down Daisy's face as she remembered how both men had laughed before leaving her trussed up on the narrow bed.

How can they do this to another human being? It's just not right.

2

D aisy woke hesitantly. The room was quiet, quieter than it had been since the men had brought her there. She opened her eyes, glancing around the small space, but didn't see anyone. She gave a mental sigh of relief. Daisy realized the ropes no longer bound her wrists to the bed's rough posts for the first time. Her wrists throbbed, and Daisy glanced down to see bloody abrasions there.

I'm gonna have to hide these. Mama will be so ashamed when she sees them.

Two weeks earlier, Daisy had been out picking berries. On her way to another patch, two men had come upon her, and this nightmare had begun. One of them had pulled her up onto his horse after distracting her with a question about how to get back to town. Daisy could remember his cackling laugh as he'd held her against his sweaty body, kneading her bosoms and her behind as she struggled in his arms. It had been so degrading and humiliating. She'd never been treated in such a manner and couldn't imagine it happening.

"Just calm down, sweetheart," he'd whispered into Daisy's ear between licking and nibbling her neck. "You're gonna love this. Me and Jake have nice big cocks, and we ain't never had no complaints from any of the ladies we've poked so far."

Daisy had smelled liquor on his breath as he spoke, and she'd cringed.

What is he talking about? Whatever it is, I don't think it's gonna be good, and I know I'm not gonna love it, no matter what he says. Mama says men with whiskey on their breath have no good on their minds.

They eventually came to an old shack on the mountainside built in the shade of pines and poplars. Daisy didn't think it looked like a house where a family lived. It had a deserted appearance, and she didn't think the weathered, silvery boards had ever seen paint.

"Hand her down to me, Jamison," Jake said after he tied his horse to a post. "I'll hang on to her while you tend to your horse. I want a feel of that nice fresh cunny, too."

Jamison dropped Daisy to the ground, and Jake wrapped his arms around her. "Feel those bosoms, Jake," Jamison cackled as he slid from the saddle. "I can't wait to get me a taste of 'em."

Jake leered down at Daisy and grabbed one of her bosoms. "Well, let's have us a look," he said and pulled at the neckline of Daisy's dress, ripping it open to expose the white cotton camisole beneath.

It took me a week to make that dress. Mama is gonna be so mad at me for lettin' it get ruined like this.

"That's pretty and all," Jamison said when he joined them after securing his mount, "but it's in the way of our fun, ain't it?" The tiny pearl buttons flew into the leaf-strewn ground as he yanked the camisole open to expose her heaving bosoms. "Now that's what I call pretty," Jamison said with a drunken laugh and bent to suck a nipple into his mouth.

He sucked hard and then bit the nipple. Daisy screamed with the pain and tried to twist out of Jake's grasp. "Let me go!" she yelled, and the two young men laughed at her distress. "Please, just let me go."

What kind of men are these?

"This one's gonna be a fighter, Jamison. You better bring your rope," Jake called, as he began to walk Daisy toward the door of the deserted shack. "You can yell all you want, girl," he said from behind Daisy, "but this here line shack ain't used much no more and is miles away from any living soul."

He kicked the door open and pushed her inside. "Holler all ya want," he said, "cause ain't no one gonna hear ya."

Tears streamed down Daisy's sunburned face as she landed hard on the dirty floor of the shack. It smelled musty and old, like her Papa's wet socks if he left them out on the porch too long before bringing them in to be washed. Webs hung from the ceiling, and Daisy shivered at the thought of spiders. She had no idea that what waited for her was much worse than spiders.

This is not gonna be good.

One of them grabbed the skirt of her dress and pulled it off over her narrow hips. The other man took her by the wrist and yanked her to her feet after taking off her boots and tossing them across the dusty room.

"Get on up here and give me a kiss, sweetheart," Jamison said and pressed his face into hers.

He smells disgusting.

She couldn't breathe as he covered her mouth with his and shoved his foul-tasting tongue between her teeth. Daisy bit down until she tasted coppery blood in her mouth.

"You bitch!" Jamison yelled and pulled his face away. He put his hand to his mouth, and Daisy saw his face grow pale when it came away bloody. "You're gonna pay for that, bitch," he shouted as he drew back his hand and punched Daisy in the face.

The punch knocked Daisy onto the bed that had served the visiting cowboys who used the shack when out checking fences and gathering strays. More punches followed to her face and body, but Daisy didn't feel them as they were delivered because the first one had knocked her out cold.

Daisy woke to find her hands tied to the bedposts above her head, and her feet tied to the ones at the foot. Her legs were spread apart, and a heavy weight held her down. Pain seared her groin, and Daisy lifted her eyes to see Jake atop her, sweating and grunting as he poked his cock between her bruised and throbbing thighs.

My first time wasn't supposed to be like this. It was supposed to be with a man... one man... a man I love, on my wedding night.

"Holy mother of God," Jake groaned as he shoved hard with his release. "You were right, Jamison," he said, looking over to his friend, who stood at the open door watching, "her cunny is tight."

"They always are when you get 'em fresh like that," Jamison said with a chuckle. "Ain't you never had a virgin before, Jake?"

He let all his weight fall onto Daisy, and she wrinkled her nose at the stench of body odor coming from his hairy armpits. Tears slipped down her cheeks again.

It wasn't supposed to be like this.

She sobbed, and Jake jumped in surprise. "She's awake."

"Good," Jamison sneered. "My cock is hard again, and I'd like to enjoy a little fight this time."

Through her tears, Daisy saw the naked young man with the hard organ in his hand, stroking it with a light touch. Jake rolled off her and stood. His flaccid cock dangled from a nest of dark blond, coarse hair, leaking sticky white fluid.

Daisy's mother had explained to her where babies came from, and she knew what leaked from the withered organ.

Oh, dear Lord, this could get me with child. I'm only nineteen and unmarried. I can't get with child yet. Mama will send me to the Magdalenes.

Jamison strode back to the bed with a grin on his face and ran a rough finger across her lips. "Which hole should we try next, I wonder?"

Daisy tried to clamp her lips closed as he pressed his cock toward it, but he grabbed a hand full of her blonde curls and twisted. "Open up, sweetheart," he sneered, "and don't even think about biting me, or what you'll get will make those love-taps I gave you before seem pale by comparison."

He rubbed his swollen cock against her lips and pulled her hair harder. "Open wide, sweetheart. I wanna feel my cock slide over your sweet little tongue."

I think I'm gonna throw up. He's so disgusting. He's made me into something vile. No man is gonna want me after this.

Daisy parted her quivering lips a little and, before she knew it, the stiff organ slid over her tongue. He pushed it in until she gagged, and Daisy heard Jake laughing from the side of the bed where he stood naked, watching.

Her eyes flew open wide when she felt Jake's fingers probing between her butt cheeks until he found the tight opening there. "I think I wanna try this one next," he said, with a cackling laugh that Jamison matched as he pumped into Daisy's mouth.

"We're gonna use all the bitch's holes," Jamison said and pushed in far enough to make Daisy gag again. "Go ahead and fill her ass, Jake. I wanna watch the little bitch lick you clean when you're done."

Daisy gagged again, but it wasn't because he'd rammed his stiff organ too far into her mouth.

He can't possibly be serious. Can he?

Jake grabbed both her legs and pulled her down as far as she could go, restrained as she was. She screamed when his cock head pushed into her tight anus. She screamed louder when he pushed fully into her.

This can't be happening. God, it hurts so much.

The excitement of her screams brought Jamison to his climax, and he filled her mouth with a stream of hot, bitter fluid. Daisy wanted it, and the wilting cock, out of her mouth, and she began pushing it out with her tongue.

Jamison's shrinking cock rubbed across Daisy's sharp, pointed eye-tooth, and he yelled. "I told you not to bite me, bitch."

More blows rained down on her face and abdomen as Jake continued to pump into the hole between her butt cheeks. Daisy lost count of the blows, and the pain consumed her abused body.

Do all men do this? Mama never told me about any of this. I can't believe she lets Papa do any of this to her.

That first night alone had been difficult, but there had been more. After three or four, Daisy lost count. It was either dark or light. She was either alone, or she wasn't. She thanked God when only the two of them showed up. Daisy didn't think she could endure more than the two of them abusing her, though Jamison continued to threaten it.

"One of these days, sweetheart," he'd whisper into her ear, "I'm gonna watch as all three of your holes are filled with cock at the same time."

The young men came and went, but they always returned to pummel her body with fists and cocks. Jake gave her water when she begged for a drink, but when she asked for something to eat, Jamison told her their cock juice was the only food she should expect, so she began to swallow the awful stuff reluctantly. They enjoyed that and used her mouth more.

At least it can't get me with child.

Daisy lost track of time. Day turned to night. They usually left during the day and allowed her to use a pan to relieve herself when they came in the evenings before taking their turns with her body. She slept while they were gone or tried to get out of the ropes binding her feet and hands. Daisy knew her wrists and ankles were raw and bleeding, but she continued to struggle.

I have to get out of here. Mama and Papa must be worried, sick. I wonder if they're out looking for me. Do they think I ran off, or if I'm lying dead somewhere?

Jake wasn't familiar to Daisy, but she recognized Jamison. He was Jamison Earl, son of the most prominent rancher in the valley. He'd gotten into some trouble last fall when he'd made inappropriate advances to Jenny Carpenter at the Harvest Dance. Mr. Earl had paid Jenny's father to drop the charges, and her father had bought her a new dress at the mercantile with some of the money. Mama had said the whole thing was Jenny's fault. If she hadn't been acting like a loose woman at the dance, it would never have happened.

Will you think this is my fault, too, Mama? Was I walking down the road, swinging my bucket of berries in a loose manner to deserve what Jamison and Jake have done to me?

Daisy dozed as the late afternoon heat warmed the shack. She woke to the pain of someone twisting her nipple. "Wake up, bitch," Jamison said as he pinched the tender pink flesh between his thumb and forefinger. "We ain't got much time this afternoon, so me and Jake are gonna both do ya at the same time."

"Filthy assholes," Daisy snarled, using obscenities she'd heard the boys at school use, and tried to twist away from him on the bed.

"Hear that, Jake?" Jamison said and twisted harder. "The little bitch says we're dirty assholes." Jamison punched her hard in the ribs. The pain caused Daisy to see stars before her eyes for a minute, but she refused to shed another tear.

I'll bear the pain, but I'll not give them the satisfaction of seeing me cry again. I'm done with that.

He unbuttoned his shirt, peeled it off his sweaty body, and kicked off his boots. "Just for that, I think I'll let the bitch lick my dirty asshole. I like a good tongue fuck from a bitch."

Oh, dear lord, what now? Does this man find pleasure in every disgusting act imaginable?

Jamison shed his trousers, jumped onto the bed, and straddled Daisy's chest, facing the foot of the bed. He backed up and shoved his ass in Daisy's face. He used his hands to spread the cheeks apart and expose his anus.

"There ya go, sweetheart," he said in a childish tone. "Now use that sweet little tongue like a cock and poke my asshole with it."

Jamison pressed his ass into her face. It didn't smell like shit as she had feared, but it did smell like sweat and body odor.

I guess I'd better do it, or he'll smother me.

Daisy lifted her head, stuck out her tongue, and flicked it over Jamison's puckered, brown asshole.

"That's nice, sweetheart," he moaned. "Now stick it in as far as you can, pull it out, and stick it in again. Poke my asshole with your tongue the way me and Jake use our cocks on yours."

Daisy stiffened her tongue and did as the hateful cowboy told her before he got angry and hurt her again with something more humiliating and painful. Jake walked around to watch as she bobbed her head to poke her tongue in and out of Jamison.

"Damned if she ain't doin' it," Jake said, as he watched, wide-eyed.

"Of course she is," Jamison said as he leaped to the floor. "Now I'm gonna return the favor. You should give it a try, Jake. It feels amazin' and will get your cock hard as a damned rock."

Jake took Jamison's place, but he put his hard cock to Daisy's battered lips. "I think I'll just have her suck me today."

"I guess she does look a little hungry," Jamison said with a chuckle as he shoved his hard cock into Daisy's ass. "She got me hard as a rock with that, though."

Jamison finished and put on his clothes. "I'll see ya down at the saloon then," he said and left the shack.

Jake fed Daisy his seed and crawled off her thin body. He shook his head in pity, got his canteen from his saddle, and put it to her lips for a drink.

The water tasted cool and sweet after their abuse and the hot day. Daisy gulped the water until Jake took the canteen away. He untied her hands and feet so she could squat over the pan and relieve her bladder. A little gas pushed Jamison's leavings from her behind. Jake laughed at the sound, and Daisy blushed.

How many more indignities can I possibly suffer?

The new pain in her side from Jamison's punch made her wince as she tried to crawl back onto the bed.

"Dear God," she groaned as she curled into a ball on her side and waited for Jake to make her move so he could retie the ropes, "just let this end." She drifted into the painlessness of sleep while she was waiting.

Daisy woke to find her hands and feet free of the ropes. She jerked her head up and looked around. She was alone, and the door of the shack stood open.

Oh, my God. Am I dreaming?

The sun was dipping below the treetops to the west, but there was still some daylight. Daisy gasped from the pain in her chest as she rolled off the bed. Her eyes darted around the empty shack, but her clothes and shoes were gone. She peeked outside but saw no waiting horses at the empty trough.

If you're going to do this, Daisy, you'd better get to it before they come back to torment you again.

Daisy took a deep breath to calm her nerves, but it brought about a painful fit of coughing, which she tried to quiet with her hand at her mouth. Daisy hurried out the door naked, into the dwindling sunlight. Her eyes darted around as she took a minute to decide which way to go. If she went to the west, she was afraid she'd run into the men, so she ran to the east into the thick pines.

Pine cones and sharp stones cut her feet, but years of walking barefoot on the farm had toughened her soles, and the sticks and stones didn't hurt as much as Jamison's punches to her belly, ribs, and face had. The evening air was cold on her bare skin, but all she could think about was escaping.

I can't believe I'm free. There has to be someone close by who can help me get home. There just has to be.

LORI BEASLEY BRADLEY

Just thinking about Jamison's vicious punches brought searing pain to Daisy's side as she ran through the dense trees. She sucked air into her throbbing lungs but couldn't get enough. Daisy wanted to cough but didn't want to slow down. If she slowed down for a coughing fit, she didn't know if she'd be able to start running again. So, Daisy ran.

I've got to keep going. If I stop now, they'll find me and take me back there, and I can't take any more of that.

She ran through brambles that cut her naked body and whipped her face, but she didn't slow. Her hair fell into her eyes and caught on low branches. Daisy's toe caught on a rock, and she fell into the dry leaves, rolling and sliding down a hill.

When she came to a stop on her belly, she glanced back up the hill. It was steep.

I don't think they'll be following me down that, and it's almost dark anyhow. Maybe the bastards won't follow me at all when they come back and find me gone.

The sound of water trickling over rocks caught Daisy's attention. Her mouth was parched, and her tongue dry as a bone. She needed a drink. She pushed aside some bushes and saw a stream. Unable to get to the water through the thick undergrowth, Daisy made her way around the bushes and finally knelt at the stream and gulped cold, sweet water from her trembling hands.

Daisy stood, and a terrible fit of coughing took her. She doubled over with the pain in her side and groaned as she did her best to suppress it and stay as quiet as she could. When the coughing fit ended, Daisy saw blood on her hand and tasted it in her mouth.

What now? Did I bite my tongue when I tumbled down that hill?

Across the stream stretched a green field of grass and flowering summer plants. Daisy suffered another violent fit of coughing, and she backed up toward the bushes where she dropped into an area covered in the thick, soft grass. The ground was still warm from the sun, though the soft grass felt cool on her aching body.

Maybe I'll just rest here for a spell.

Exhausted from the abuse, the run, and the coughing, Daisy snuggled into the soft grass and fell into a deep sleep.

14

3

The sun was high in the blue sky when Daisy woke and stood. She took a deep breath, surprised to feel no pain in her chest or side.

Maybe I just needed a good night's sleep out in the fresh air to regain my strength.

The bright sun blinded her as Daisy peered across the green field of swaying grass and spring wildflowers. She squinted and began to march through the knee-high grass toward the house she thought she saw in the distance. If she could get there, maybe someone could help her get home to her parents.

Mama and Papa must be worried sick after all this time. I've got to try and get back home.

Voices yelling behind her forced Daisy into a run. She wasn't hurting anymore, so she ran faster. The house and barn became clearer, and it encouraged her to move more quickly. The weeds and grass in the field didn't hurt her feet as the forest floor had, and it lifted Daisy's heart a bit.

The sun was low in the western sky when she finally reached the neat farmhouse with a white picket fence around a trimmed, green front yard.

I don't have a thing on. What are these folks gonna think of me? Maybe they'll understand when I explain, but I hope there aren't any children here. I must look frightful with all these bruises.

Daisy didn't see or hear anybody around the house. No chickens were clucking in the neat yard, or dogs barking at the arrival of a stranger. Daisy listened but didn't hear any cows out back, either. Perhaps the family had gone to town and put the stock up in the big barn. She didn't even know what day it was. If it was Sunday, the family had probably gone to church.

Pushing aside thoughts of her nakedness, Daisy opened the gate and stepped onto the sun-warmed, stone pathway, leading to a tidy porch with turned posts painted white. She knocked on the door, but no one answered. Daisy knocked again and waited.

As she was about to knock again, the door creaked open, and Daisy peered into the dark house.

That's strange. Maybe it didn't catch well when the family left.

"Hello," she called. "Is anyone here?"

Nobody answered her call, so Daisy stepped inside. A bright front room greeted her, with comfortable furniture. With her heart pounding in her chest, Daisy made her way through the tidy room until she came to a spacious kitchen where a big pine table stood with benches on either side. The room smelled of bacon fat, and she marveled at a large work island, a nice stove, and many cabinets.

This is some kitchen. A big family must live here. I wonder where they are.

A clock chimed, and Daisy flinched in surprise.

To her left, she saw stairs leading to the upper floor and a large bedroom. Daisy crept into the darkening room, nervous about being in someone else's house, but glad to be away from Jamison and Jake. The large bed was made up but, exhausted from her run across the field, Daisy pulled the quilt aside and crawled beneath.

I never thought I'd be comfortable in a bed again, but this feels so nice.

Daisy snuggled into the soft pillow, closed her eyes, and allowed sleep to take her.

———————

From behind the front door, Carl Emmons watched the pretty, naked girl wander through his house.

Where the hell are her clothes? She looks frightful with all those bruises. I wonder what happened to her.

He followed quietly behind her as she studied the kitchen, peered up the stairs, and then wandered into his bedroom. It had been a good while since any woman had been in his house, especially a pretty one without any clothes.

I hope you don't blame me for lookin', Mercy. She's a pretty little thing, and you're the one who left me here all alone.

Carl followed the young blonde into the dark bedroom. He could hear her soft, even breathing and knew the girl was sleeping. He took a deep breath and ran a hand through his dark curls. Carl wrinkled his nose as the rank scent of the sleeping girl's body odor reached him.

He stretched his tall, lean body before dropping into the rocking chair beside the west window where Mercy had rocked their babies and settled them to sleep after nursing. Carl clenched his hands on the old chair's smooth arms and frowned as he stared at the sleeping form on his bed in Mercy's spot.

Don't be mad, Mercy. I didn't invite her in.

Outside, the wind began to howl as a storm settled over the valley. Lightning flashed, and thunder rattled the windows. Carl glanced up, but the sleeping girl never noticed the commotion outside. Rain pelted the glass beside him as Carl's head drooped onto his chest, and he joined the softly snoring girl in sleep.

———

Daisy's head jerked up when she felt the weight of somebody settling on the bed beside her, and her eyes flew open. Her heart thudded in her chest as she saw a man in a blue cotton shirt staring down at her.

"Good morning," he said awkwardly. "I hope you slept well."

As she clutched the quilt at her throat with trembling fingers, Daisy's eyes darted around her surroundings. Morning light streamed in to brighten the room.

"I'm sorry, sir," she gasped uneasily and sat up. "I didn't mean to trespass, but I need help to get home."

Oh, dear lord. I'm lyin' here naked in a strange man's bed. What must he think of me?

Carl grinned down at the girl. "I'm gonna fix us some breakfast," he said and turned toward the kitchen. "There's water in the pitcher on the washstand. Why don't you wash yourself up? There are clothes that will probably fit you in the wardrobe over there." He walked out of the room. "You're welcome to 'em. There's no one here to wear 'em anymore."

Daisy continued to lie motionless until she heard him rummaging in the kitchen. When she smelled bacon frying, she finally pushed the blanket aside and went to the washbasin, where she found warm water in an enameled, white pitcher.

I'm sure I can use a bath. I don't even have any idea how long it's been, and those men had their stinking bodies upon me for all that time.

Daisy poured it into the bowl, found a cloth with a ball of sweet-smelling soap, and made quick work of washing her bruised body and matted hair. The scent of the soap filled her nose, and Daisy smiled. She loved roses.

At least I don't hurt the way I did, but what's he gonna think when he sees these rope burns on my wrists and ankles?

On one side of the wardrobe, Daisy found dresses hanging, along with some camisoles and petticoats. She slipped into the white cotton underthings and then chose a blue calico dress with long sleeves. It was a little big and brushed the floor, but Daisy was glad to be covered again. The woman they belonged to had obviously been bigger than her.

She buttoned the cuffs, concealing the angry red welts on her wrists, and gazed down at the floor, glad he wouldn't be able to see the ones on her ankles, either. Daisy padded into the kitchen, where the man was slicing bread at the work island. A platter of crisp fried bacon was set on the table, along with two plates and cups filled with hot coffee.

"Have a seat," the man said, as he turned to drop the bread slices onto the stovetop to warm and brown. "My name is Carl, by the way, Carl Emmons. Who are you?"

"Daisy Dale," she said as she sat down. "My Papa is Henry Dale. We live over by Butte Creek, north of town."

Carl turned to her and smiled. "I know an Everett Dale who lives over that way. Might you be related?"

Daisy frowned and picked up the cup of coffee. "Everett was my grandpa," she said, "but he passed over a year ago."

Carl turned the bread. "I'm sorry," he said. "I hadn't heard, but I've been busy here on the farm and haven't been into town much in the past year."

That's odd. I thought everybody hereabouts knew about Grandpa fallin' off ol' Blue and breakin' his neck.

"I didn't even know Everett was married and had children," Carl said, "much less growed-up grandchildren."

"Papa is from his first wife back in Missouri," Daisy said, as Carl brought the toasted bread to the table. "He and Mama married back there, and we came out here after Papa got word my grandpa had died and left him the farm. We've only been here a little less than a year."

"Oh, I see," Carl said and picked up his coffee. "I guess that's why I never met your papa."

"This is a real nice house," Daisy said, and she glanced down at the dress she had on. "Your wife must love this kitchen. I hope she won't mind me wearin' one of her dresses."

Daisy watched his face darken as he pulled the crock of jam toward him and scooped some out. "She don't live here anymore. She up and left me a while back and took my children with her." He pushed the crock to Daisy.

"I'm so very sorry," Daisy said and scooped some of the jam onto her toasted bread. "Do you know where they went? Not that it's any of my business, of course."

Carl flashed her a weak grin. "It's all right. She probably went back to her pa's," he said as he bit into his toast. "The old man never liked me and tried to talk Mercy out of marryin' me. He never thought I'd be able to make a go of this place. It was just bare land when me and Mercy came here, but we worked hard and built it all up from nothin'."

Poor man. I wonder why she left such a lovely place. He seems nice, and he's certainly better looking than some I've seen. I wonder how close this place is to ours. I've never heard anyone mention the Emmons family before, but I don't socialize as much as some.

4

Henry and Lola Dale stood before those assembled at the Paradice Baptist Church. Lola wrung her hands with her eyes rimmed red from hours of worry and tears, while her husband stood with his hand on the small of her back for support.

"I wanna thank all y'all for comin' out in our time of need," Henry said in a strong, firm voice. "Most of you know our Daisy. She's a good girl and just passed the exams to become a teacher."

Lola stared out at the crowd. Most looked at them with sadness and pity in their eyes, but Lola noted a few who appeared skeptical. A nineteen-year-old girl doesn't simply disappear. She must have run off with a man.

We should never have come to this God-forsaken place. There's nothing here but illiterate ranchers and their equally illiterate wives and children. What kind of place is this to raise a daughter? What future is there for her here? We should have stayed in St. Louis, where she could have gone to a good school with the prospects of finding a good husband.

As Henry went on thanking the church members and the community, the doors of the building pushed open, and Marshal Ken Reese and his men walked in. The tall, handsome Marshal took off his hat as he strode up the center aisle between the rows of pews. The members of his posse who had family there joined their wives and children.

"Did you find her?" Lola asked as she held her husband's hand.

"I'm sorry, ma'am," Marshal Reese said in his deep voice, "we didn't."

Lola wept as she heard a groan from the crowd. "My poor baby," she sobbed into her husband's shoulder. "What could have happened to her?"

Marshal Reese turned to the people assembled in the pews. "We aren't giving up the search, ma'am," he called, as his eyes settled on Lola, "but it's dark now, and everybody is tired. We'll meet again at my office in the morning and spread out into areas we haven't searched yet. This is a big county."

"Thank you, Marshal," Henry said, extending his trembling hand to the tall lawman. "You didn't find any sign of my girl?"

Marshal Reese shook his head. "Nothing since that first day when we found that bucket of berries out on the mill road."

"But how could she have just disappeared?" Henry asked as he held his sobbing wife.

"Henry," the Marshal sighed, "I just don't know, sir. There were tracks on the road by where we found the bucket, but there's no way of knowing who left them, or even when."

"We know, Marshal," Lola sobbed, "but please don't give up looking."

Marshal Reese patted the sobbing woman on the shoulder. "We won't, ma'am. We'll keep looking until we find her and bring her home to you and Mr. Dale."

He thinks she's dead or run off with a man like a common tramp. If that's the case, I'd just as soon he brings us her body. If she's run off with one of these silly cowhands, I don't think I could bear the shame of it all.

"Thank you again, Marshal," Henry said and wrapped his arm around his wife's slumped shoulders. "Come on, Mama, let's get you home so you can rest."

Lola couldn't look at the faces of the women as she allowed her husband to usher her up the aisle toward the door of the little church.

"I don't know," Lola heard Myrtle Biggs say to her daughter as they passed, "why we're spending all this time and energy looking for a little tart who probably ran off with one of those cowboys who were through town last week with that drive."

I know that's what they're all thinking, and if that's what happened, I hope she never comes back.

In the Pair O' Dice Saloon, a half-mile from the church, Jamison Earl sat at a table with three of his friends and a bottle of whiskey. Molly, the waitress, had just wriggled out of his grasp, and his friends laughed.

"I don't need the haughty little bitch anyhow." Jamison scowled after Molly as she scooted back to the bar with an empty bottle in her hand. "I got better up at the line shack waitin' for me to get back."

"Oh, yeah?" one of the men at the table cackled. "Who's that?"

Jamison raised a brow and smiled as he filled his glass with the amber liquid. "Just don't you never mind who, Paul," he said with a grin, "but she's got the sweetest little cunny and tightest little asshole you ever poked a cock in."

"Sure, she does," taunted another, "and she gives it all to ya?"

"That and her mouth, too, Brad," Jamison bragged. "She begs Jake and me to put it to her every time we visit her up there."

"Is it someone we know?" one of the men asked. "Maybe we've already had a taste."

"Nope, Doug," Jamison howled, "I was the first one in her tight little cunny, and Jake was the first one in her ass." He emptied his glass. "I can't rightly remember who she sucked first, though, but she does it nice and swallows every drop we give her."

"Where'd ya find such a jewel?" Brad asked as he stretched in his chair. "You wouldn't be of a mind to share, would ya? I ain't had my cock sucked in a while."

Jamison filled his glass again as he considered. "Jake was in her mouth when I left 'em this afternoon, but he's probably done with her by now."

"And she just waits up there at the shack for ya?" Paul asked incredulously.

"We got the little cunny tied to the damned bed," Jamison laughed. "She can't get away. She's our private stock to play with at our leisure." He downed another glass as men in the saloon looked on.

"I knew she was gonna be sweet when we saw her strollin' down that road swingin' a bucket in her hand and her blonde curls blowin' in the breeze." He chuckled. "And she was, too. She screamed a bit when I poked her that first time," Jamison said with a broad smile and cackled, "but you shoulda heard her howl when Jake filled her damned asshole the first time."

"I ain't poked an ass since we plugged that little whore down in Bridgeport last summer," Doug sighed. "I could sure use a little of that tonight."

Jamison stared around the table, threw back his drink, and slammed the glass on the table as he stood. "Well, come on then, fellas. We can wake the little bitch up, and all get us a taste. I think my cock can get hard again."

Brad and Doug stood, but Paul remained seated. "You fellas go on," he sighed. "I gotta be at the mill early in the mornin'."

"Your loss," Jamison chuckled as he put his arms around the other two men's shoulders and left the smoky saloon.

Tom Harding left the busy saloon and ran to the church. He saw Lola and Henry walking toward their buggy.

"Wait a minute, Henry," he called, waving his arms frantically to get the couple's attention. "I might have news."

Henry helped Lola up into the buggy and stood while the tall, gaunt man came running. "What do you know, Tom? Has someone found our Daisy?"

Tom glanced up at Lola's tear-streaked face and pulled Henry away from the buggy, a few steps toward the group of people exiting the church.

"I just came from the Pair O' Dice, and Jamison Earl was in there goin' on about him and Jake Morgan havin' a girl tied up at some line shack."

Henry grabbed Tom's slender arm. "Did he say it was Daisy?" Henry turned to his wife. "Tom might know where our Daisy is, Mama."

"Where is she, Tom?" a woman from the church called. "Is she all right?"

Tom shrugged his skeletal shoulders. "I guess she's been with Jamison Earl and Jake Morgan up in one of the Earl line shacks," Tom said to the assembling crowd.

"Out whorin' like the little tart I knew she was all along," Myrtle Biggs yelled. "Me and mine ain't givin' no more of our time or energy to this hunt," she huffed. "We've been cookin' for days to feed men that were out lookin' for this missing little tart." She put her arm around the shoulders of her young daughter and marched her away from the church.

Tom stood with his mouth open, his eyes darting between Henry, Lola, and the departing woman. "I'm sorry, Henry," he stammered. "I didn't mean to say Daisy was there of her own accord."

Henry glanced at his appalled wife, then patted Tom's shoulder. "I know, Tom. Thanks for the information. We'll pass it on to the Marshal."

"Good," Tom said with a relieved sigh. He turned and doffed his hat to Lola. "Ma'am."

Henry climbed into the buggy. "We should go to the Marshal with this right now."

"No," Lola snapped. "Take me home."

"But…" Henry attempted.

"But nothing, Henry. The girl's disgraced us, running off to spread her legs in a filthy line shack for not one man," Lola sobbed, "but two, like a common mine camp whore." She straightened in the buggy seat and stared straight ahead into the darkness. "Just take me home."

———

Paul waited until he heard their horses trot away before leaving the saloon. He walked briskly down the boardwalk until he came to the door he wanted and began to knock, pounding his fist on the wood until he saw the glow of a lamp inside.

"*What?*" bellowed Marshal Reese when he pulled open the door, wearing only his white cotton long johns. The tall Marshal glared down at the shorter man and rubbed his eyes. "Adams? What the hell do you want at this hour?"

"I think I might know where that little Dale gal is, Marshal," Paul said, breathless from the fast walk down the boardwalk.

The Marshal raised an eyebrow and stepped aside. "Come on in, then, and tell me what you know. We've been out searchin' the hills for two weeks now and had no sign of her."

Paul stepped inside, and Marshal Reese closed the door. "I was down at the Pair O' Dice," Paul said, "and Jamison Earl was in there, shootin' his mouth off."

"When is he not?" Reese said, rolling his sleepy blue eyes. "Have a seat," he told Paul and pointed to a chair at a table in the center of the office. "What did the moron have to say about the girl?"

Paul took a deep breath and removed his hat. "I don't know for certain he was talkin' about her, but he said him and Jake Morgan picked up a girl and have her tied up in a line shack that belongs to the Earl Ranch. He says they've been using her like a whore."

Marshal Reese's face grew darker with that. "What made you think it was the Dale girl and not a gal from a saloon somewhere?"

"I heard tell you found a bucket on the road where she disappeared?" Paul said.

"Yep," he said, "out on the mill road."

"And she's a gal with curly blonde hair?" Paul continued.

Marshal Reese nodded. "She is."

Paul ran a hand through his thin hair. "That arrogant ass said him, and Jake grabbed up a blonde gal who was walking down a road with a bucket in her hand. Don't that sound like her to you?"

"And he told you where they took her?" Reese asked, getting up to put some coffee on the stove.

Paul nodded. "An old line shack up on Earl's west ridge.

"I think I know the one," the Marshal sighed. "I've chased drunken cowboys out of there a time or two with silly little gals they had no business bein' up there with."

Paul grinned. "That's the one, but this time I don't think the little gal went of her own accord with girlish notions of romance in her silly head."

Marshal Reese yawned as he got up and poured coffee into two stoneware cups. "If we leave right away, I think we can get up there before daylight."

"Jamison is on his way up there with two fellas from here in town. He promised 'em a go at her," Paul said uneasily, as he took the offered cup.

"Oh, good lord," Reese sighed as he sat again. "That boy's daddy didn't whip his ass nearly enough, but if I get the chance, I certainly will take the opportunity to make up for his lacking."

Paul drained his cup and stood. "I'm ready whenever you are, Marshal."

5

"This is a beautiful farm, Carl," Daisy said as she walked beside the handsome farmer.

He'd just shown her the barn where a cow awaited her afternoon milking. Her yearling calf grazed in the fenced acre outside beneath peach and plum trees heavy with fruit.

"Thank you," he said, smiling down at her as they walked back toward the house. "It's been a lot of work, but…" His voice trailed off, and Daisy thought she saw profound sadness in his handsome hazel eyes. "I thought to leave it to my son." He stopped and choked back a sob.

Daisy touched his arm with hesitation, his sob bringing her to the brink of tears. "I'm so sorry, Carl. I didn't mean to fret you none."

Carl wiped his face with his sleeve and took a deep breath before unlatching the gate into the green yard. He glanced down at Daisy and smiled. "It's none of your doin'," he sighed. "Mercy changed after the birth of our last boy." They walked through the gate, and Carl closed it behind them. "She had the blues some after birthin' the other three, but she was especially sad after him, and she couldn't seem to shake it no matter what I did."

"I've heard tell that can happen with some women," Daisy said sympathetically, as they moved toward the house again.

"One day, she just up and took the children away." He ran a hand through his thick brown curls and exhaled a long sigh. "Took 'em to her pa's ranch up on the Feather River, I suppose."

"You never went to look for them?" Daisy asked, enjoying the feel of the soft, cool grass on her bare feet.

I can't imagine wanting to leave a lovely farm like this. It has everything a woman could possibly want.

Daisy had marveled at the kitchen but had been equally impressed with the big washhouse where a woman could do her laundry out of the elements in the winter months. It even had a stove for heating wash water and keeping the room warm and dry when it was too cold to hang the wash on the line outside.

Beneath the washhouse, in relatively close proximity to the kitchen door, was a neat and tidy cellar with shelves on one wall for canned produce and bins of straw for root vegetables.

Rose bushes, peonies, and other flowers dotted the neat yard. Tall maples shaded the lawn where plump white hens roamed, and a well-tended garden grew to the west end of the property. Daisy thought the house, garden, barn lot, and cow pasture must sit on ten acres, with another twenty or thirty to the north and east planted with tall, green stalks of corn.

This farm is absolutely heavenly. What woman would want to leave it?

Carl sighed again and shrugged. "It was her decision. If she's happy somewhere else, I wish her well. I couldn't have tended four young'uns here alone and farmed too, so I suppose it's for the best."

They came upon a small area fenced with white pickets and peony plants. Inside, Daisy saw a tall marker. A chill ran down her spine as she recognized a family grave plot.

"Did you and your wife lose a child, Carl?" Daisy asked as they passed the fence.

Carl glanced at the marker and quickly averted his eyes. "It belonged to the family who lived here before Mercy and me," he said, as they continued to the house.

I thought he said he and his wife built this place from the ground up. Maybe someone else was here first and got it started.

By the time they got back into the house, the sun was setting behind the tall Sierra Nevada Mountains to the west.

"Would you allow me to cook supper for you?" Daisy asked.

Carl smiled. "That would be right nice of ya. There's a ham in the icebox."

Daisy had heard tell of the amazing devices that would keep food cool and retard spoilage, but she'd never seen one.

He must have truly loved that woman to have supplied her with such modern accessories in her kitchen. I can't fathom a woman wanting to leave that.

Daisy busied herself in the opulent kitchen and made them a supper of sliced ham, mashed potatoes, cream gravy, biscuits, and fresh tomatoes from the garden.

"This was a fine meal," Carl said as he stood. "I'll fetch ya some water for the dishes."

"Thank you," she said, stacking the pretty china plates to carry to the sink.

They'd had china dishes when they lived in St. Louis, as well as nice furniture and fancy clothes. They'd sold most of it before traveling to California. There wasn't room in the wagon for oak highboys, wardrobes, long settees, or trunks full of fine clothes they'd never have a use for away from the city.

Papa had assured them his father's house would be furnished with everything they would need. Daisy smiled, remembering the look of horror on her Mama's face when they'd first walked into her grandfather's stark cabin, which had been ransacked and left virtually empty after his death. All that had remained was a table and two broken chairs in the kitchen, which was stripped of its stove, dishes, and cooking pots.

It had taken them weeks to set things right and purchase a new stove. Papa and Mama had their bed from the wagon, but Daisy had slept on a pallet on the floor of the small second bedroom. Papa mended the chairs, and they brought in things from the wagon they'd brought from St. Louis. Mama had refused to part with her oak sideboard, but they had nothing but enameled tin dishes to store in it.

A family of racoons had to be chased from the chimney before they could build a fire in the fireplace. Mama had dropped to the floor and cried after the cabin filled with smoke on the first attempt to use the fireplace to make coffee. Mama had never been one for adventures, and their trek across the country had certainly been an adventure.

The long trip to California had been hardest on Mama. She hadn't wanted to leave St. Louis and their big, comfortable house on Tucker Street. Her family, German immigrants, owned a large brewery in the city and were quite well-off. They had frowned on their youngest daughter marrying a poor dockworker from a broken family, but Mama had always been headstrong. The fact that her mother already carried Daisy in her belly had made the marriage all the easier for them to accept.

I doubt I'll ever marry now. What man would want a soiled woman like me? I probably won't even be able to get a position teaching now. What family is going to want a soiled woman like me teaching their child?

When Daisy had finished the dishes and wiped down the kitchen, Carl picked up the lantern, took her hand, and led her up the narrow stairs.

"This room here," he said and motioned to the large open space to the left of the stairs, "was where my girls Sadie and Laura slept."

A large four-poster bed sat beside the only window in the room. Daisy saw two fat feather pillows with fancy embroidered pillowslips and a quilt tacked with red yarn on the bed.

"That," he said and pointed to a closed door on the right, "was Mercy's sewing room." He walked past without opening the door.

She even had a sewing room? What woman walks away from that?

At the back of the railing around the stairwell hung a wooden rod, and from the rod hung dresses and petticoats belonging to little girls, as well as shirts belonging to little boys.

Past the clothes, Carl opened another door. "This room belonged to my boy, Tommy. The baby still slept in the room downstairs with us, but we would have moved him up here when he was big enough. There's a grate in the floor, so heat from the kitchen can warm it in the cold months." He pointed to the curtainless window. "That window faces north and gets a nice breeze in the warmer months." He paused, giving Daisy a searching look.

"I'll leave it to you to choose," he said finally, as he lit a lamp beside another four-poster bed. "You're welcome to stay as long as you like, Daisy."

He patted her shoulder, and she flinched at his touch. He pulled his hand away and turned to leave the room. "I'll bring you a nightdress and some water for the washbasin. The chamber pot under the bed is clean."

"Thank you, Carl," Daisy said, as the handsome man left the room.

I don't know him well, but I can't fathom a woman leaving a man like that or a lovely house like this.

6

Marshal Reese and Paul Adams rode up the mountain to the line shack owned by the Earl Ranch. Three horses stood outside, and the flickering glow of a lantern showed through the open door.

The Marshal pulled his big dun to a halt a hundred yards from the shack and dismounted. "We'll leave the horses here and walk," he told Paul in a hushed tone.

Paul nodded and joined the Marshal on the ground. They tied the horses to trees and crept through the fallen pine needles to the shack.

"I don't know where she could be," they heard Jamison lamenting as they neared.

"I think you was imaginin' her all this time," Paul heard Doug's deep voice say, before chuckling.

Paul followed the Marshal to the door to peek in. The three men had their backs turned away from the open door.

Jamison picked up the ropes from the soiled mattress. "No, these are the ropes we had her tied up with," he protested, tossing the ropes to one of the men. "You can even see the blood where she rubbed herself raw tryin' to get loose."

"Looks like she got loose," Paul heard Brad snort. "You must not have tied her too good, Earl."

"I told ya Jake was pokin' the little bitch when I left," Jamison snarled. "He musta let her loose to use the pot and let her get away." Jamison began to laugh. "She won't get far in the dark, though, and where would she go? She's naked as a jaybird and ain't got no shoes. I took those and burned 'em the first night."

With that, Marshal Reese cleared his throat and stepped inside the shack. "Who's naked, Jamison?"

The three young men gave a start and turned at hearing the Marshal's deep voice behind them.

"Nobody you'd know, Marshal," Jamison said, tossing the bloody ropes back on the bed. "Just a little whore from Bridgeport that me and Jake brought up here to have a little private fun with."

Marshal Reese pushed the men aside and picked up the discarded ropes. He held them to the lamp and frowned at the bright red blood soaked into the twisted jute fibers. "You got a whore to come all the way up here from Bridgeport to be tied up and poked by you and Jake Morgan?"

Jamison grinned up at the taller Marshal cockily. "Whores do what they're paid to do, Marshal."

"I'm sure payin' is the only way you could get a woman to do anything with you, Earl," the Marshal snorted, as he stuffed the ropes into the waistband of his trousers.

Paul stepped into the shack for the first time. He watched Jamison's mouth lose its grin and fall open as the color drained from his face.

"I told him every disgusting thing you said, Jamison," Paul said. "He knows you had that little Dale gal up here and that she didn't come willingly."

"What, Dale gal?" Jamison sneered. "Ain't no gal here now, though, is there?" He tried to push past the big Marshal but didn't get far before the taller man snatched the back of his shirt and pulled him back. "Let go of me, Marshal. You got no call puttin' hands on me."

"Jamison Earl," the Marshal growled, as he wrenched the young man's hands behind him and wrapped rope around them, "you're under arrest."

"What the hell for?" Jamison snarled as he tried to squirm from the Marshal's grasp. "Pokin' a dirty little whore? That ain't no crime here in

Butte County." He yelped as Marshal Reese tied Jamison's hands behind his back. "Ride to the ranch, boys," Jamison ordered Doug and Brad, "and tell my daddy this bastard has me in the Paradice jail for no good reason."

"Don't be in too big a hurry," Marshal Reese told them as he hustled Jamison out of the line shack, "I'll be out to the ranch come mornin' to have a little chat with Jake and Jamison's daddy, too." He blew out the lantern and then turned to Paul. "Get our horses while I get this little snot in his saddle."

"Sure, Marshal," Paul said and trotted off through the fragrant pines. The stench of the sweat-soaked mattress and dirty chamber pot in the shack had been overpowering, and Paul was glad to be outside in the fresh air.

Marshal Reese yanked Jamison up by the back of his denim trousers in such a way that the seam dug painfully into his tender bollocks, and he yelped in pain.

"You're gonna pay for that, Reese," Jamison snarled as he settled gingerly into his saddle. "My daddy will have your badge for puttin' hands on me like that."

"Shut up, boy, or I'll gag you with your dirty socks," Marshal Reese said and grinned as the young man glared down at him from the saddle but remained silent.

The ride into Paradice was quiet. They reached town as the sun peeked over the mountains to the east.

"I'm gonna head home now, Marshal," Paul said. "Is there anything else I can do?"

"No, Paul," Marshal Reese said, as he pulled a dozing Jamison from his saddle. "The search posse will be here in another couple of hours, and thanks to you, I'll have a better idea of where to send 'em to look. Thank you for all your help."

7

Marshal Reese slept soundly for two hours in his clothes until pounding on his door woke him. He trudged to the door, expecting a dozen men with their horses, but he only saw half that many.

Ken Reese ran a hand through his hair and stared up and down the dusty main street of Paradice. When he'd been offered the Deputy U.S. Marshal position in northern California, he'd hoped to be posted in Sacramento or Virginia City. Tiny Paradice had not even been a consideration, but here he was and in the middle of the search for a missing girl, with the son of the wealthiest rancher in the territory in his little jail. As his gal at the time had noted, "What did he expect for three dollars a month?"

"Where is everyone?" Reese asked, running a big hand through his thick brown curls to put them in order.

Ray Curry scratched his stubbled chin and frowned. "Word got around the gal's been up at some line shack whorin' herself to Jamison Earl and Jake Morgan," he sighed, "and the other fellas wouldn't come today."

Reese groaned. "That Dale girl didn't sneak up the mountain like that Biggs girl with Simon Wallace. Those men snatched her off the road and kept her tied up, doing God only knows what to her."

"We figured as much," Curry said and nodded toward the other men. "Half the men in Butte County have been in the Biggs girl's playground, and I ain't never heard nothin' like that about Miss Dale."

"Let's be on our way then," the Marshal called as he put on his hat and got on his horse. "Do all of you know where the line shack is?"

"The general area," Curry said and rode close to the Marshal's horse.

"Okay," Reese called to the other men. "We'll pair up and take the areas surrounding the shack. I want that whole mountain searched from the shack down to the base."

"Jamison said she's not wearing any clothes or shoes, so she's probably cut up and cold," the Marshal said. "Make sure to search any cliffs or gullies you come upon. The girl was wandering around out there in the dark and could have fallen."

"Sure, Marshal," Curry said. "I'll pair up with you as I seem to be the odd man today."

"I think I have something over here, Marshal," Curry called, and the Marshal maneuvered his horse through the trees to the spot where Curry knelt, studying the ground.

"What ya got?"

Curry pointed to an area of scuffed-up pine needles. "I think she may have run this way. I've been seeing tracks like this for a ways now and several broken, low-hanging branches and bushes. Somebody passed through this way at a run. I'm certain of that."

The Marshal smiled. "I'll follow you, Ray," he said and motioned for Curry to push ahead.

They followed the trail until they got to a steep drop, where a roll down the hill was evident by a scattering of leaves and pine mulch.

"I don't see any sign of her down there," Curry said and then pointed to a break in the dense foliage. "Maybe she slipped through there to get to the creek. I hope she wasn't hurt after takin' that tumble."

"Let's go see," the Marshal said. "I think we can get the horses down easier if we lead them around that way." He pointed to the north, where the ground sloped more gently toward the creek and the land beyond.

The two men led their skittish mounts between the pines, following the easy slope until they came to the break in the bushy willows growing along the slow-moving creek. They passed between two clumps of foliage and came out into the sun, where water flowed gently over moss-covered stones.

"Let's follow the creek a bit," Curry suggested, and Reese motioned for him to take the lead.

About thirty yards up the watery trail, Curry came to a stop and groaned. He pointed to something nestled against the tree-line. "Somethin's over there, Marshal."

They picked their way through the knee-high grass and weeds until they came to the still form curled in a deer wallow between the creek and a row of bushes.

Both men knelt. Marshal Reese reached out to touch cold, lifeless skin.

"Is it her?" Curry asked.

"I think so," Marshal Reese said, striding to his horse for a blanket.

He covered the body before gently lifting her into his arms. "Go round up the other fellas, Ray, while I ride back into town with her." He handed the bundle to a wide-eyed Curry while he got onto his horse.

"What ya gonna do with the poor little thing?" Curry said as he handed the blanketed form up to the Marshal. "She don't weigh nothin'."

"I'll take her to the doc's," Reese said, as he settled the body in front of him in the saddle.

Curry frowned. "Don't rightly think the doc can do much for her now."

"He can tell me what caused her death and help me decide who's responsible." Marshal Reese urged his horse forward but stopped. "You know Henry, don't you?"

"From church and runnin' into him at the feed store, is all," Curry replied, with a shrug of his slumped shoulders.

"Go by his place and ask him to come to my office, will you?"

"Aw, Marshal," Curry groaned, "you can't ask me to give a man news like this." He stared at the blanket draped across the Marshal's lap with a tuft of matted blonde curls escaping from it.

"I'll give him the news, Ray," the Marshal said. "I just need you to ask him to come in."

"Oh, okay," Curry said with a relieved sigh. "I 'spose I can do that for ya."

"Thank you," the Marshal said and then resumed his trek back toward Paradice.

"Oh lord," Doc Sterling groaned when Marshal Reese walked into his office carrying the bundled body in his arms. "I hope that's not her."

The white-headed doctor stepped aside while the big Marshal put the bundle on his exam table.

"I've only seen the girl in passing a few times," Marshal Reese sighed, "and she was dressed, but I'm fairly certain it's her." Reese took a deep breath. "She looked to be beat bad, Doc, but she likely took a bad fall out there in the dark, too. Will you be able to tell the difference?"

The old doctor gave the tall man a scathing glance. "I've been doctorin' for almost thirty years, young man. I think I can discern a bruise made by a punch from a bruise made in a tumble."

He lifted the blanket from the body and handed it to the Marshal. Doc Sterling grimaced when he pushed the blonde curls away from the girl's bruised face. "These bruises on her face are several days... more than a week old, maybe." He shook his head when he studied the rope burns on her wrists and ankles. "Looks to me like she put up a hell of a fight."

"Is it the Dale girl?" Marshal Reese asked, brushing more hair from the girl's battered face.

"It's her," the doctor affirmed sadly. "Has anybody sent for her folks?"

Reese nodded. "I sent Ray Curry to ask Henry to come to my office."

"I'll get her cleaned up." Doc Sterling sighed and glanced at the clock on his desk. "It'll take me about an hour to give you a definitive cause of death, though, so don't bring him up here before three this afternoon."

"Sure thing, Doc," Reese said as he tucked the blanket under his arm.

"I hope you've got the bastard, Ken, because scum who'd do this shouldn't be walkin' the streets of Paradice," the doctor hissed as he continued examining the body.

"One of 'em," the Marshal said, "and I'm goin' after the other one now."

Marshal Reese secured the blanket on his horse then walked back to his office to find a group of men waiting outside.

A tall, grey-headed man in a fine suit stepped forward with a frown on his face. "It's about time you got here, Marshal. I demand to see my son." Emmett Earl, the most prominent landowner around Paradice, scowled at the Marshal. "I don't even understand why you're holding him." Earl pulled a young man beside him. "Jake here says they had a little whore up at the shack, but there's no law against that."

Reese glared at Jake Morgan. "Just a whore, Jake?"

"Yeah, a sweet little cunny from down at Bridgeport."

"One that liked being tied to the bed while you used her?" the Marshal asked as he unlocked the door.

"Don't know as she liked it," Jake said with a nervous chuckle, "but that's what Jamison paid her to do."

"Then, can you explain why we found the Dale girl's body up there today with rope burns on her wrists and ankles?"

"Her... her body?" Jake stammered, taking a step back toward the door.

Marshal Reese grabbed Jake before he could flee. "You can join your friend in the back," he said and yanked Jake toward the cells.

"I demand to see my son!" Emmett Earl yelled again. "I've hired Mason Howl to represent him in this matter."

"Judge Timmons is due in town next week," the Marshal said, as he pushed Jake through the door to the cells. "You can see him before the hearing.

"What?" Earl yelled. "Mason, that's ridiculous. I want my boy home tonight."

"I'm sorry, Mr. Earl, but the Marshal can hold the boys until Judge Timmons decides to set bail or not," Howl informed him.

"Daddy!" Jamison called from the back, rattling the iron door of his cage. "Get me out of here, Daddy. We just poked a little filthy farmgirl cunny, and she liked it. She begged us to..."

Marshal Reese slammed the door, cutting off Jamison's rant. "Another five minutes, and he might have admitted killing her, too," the Marshal said and winked at the pale lawyer before turning to Emmett Earl. "I'll send word when Judge Timmons gets into town, Emmett."

At two in the afternoon, Marshal Reese returned to Doc Sterling's office.

"I thought I told you not to bring Henry up here until at least three," the old doctor growled.

"He's in my office," the Marshal said. "First, I wanted to hear what you had to say about what caused her death."

"That's easy enough," the doctor sighed and folded a white sheet off the girl's freshly-washed, pale body. "Somebody punched her in the side hard enough to break a rib, and it punctured her left lung." Doc Sterling took a shuddering breath. "The poor girl drowned in her own blood."

"Is that all?" Reese asked, staring at the sheeted body.

"No," the doctor snapped and slowly shook his head. "The bastard beat her and assaulted her in ways you can't imagine. The poor thing must have been in terrible pain for days before she died." He lifted the sheet from her abused feet and pointed at several cuts. "She ran without regard for the pain. She must have been scared to death."

"Scared to be tied up again back in that damned shack," the Marshal hissed. He ran a finger over the red abrasion on her ankle. "Can you match this to the rope that made it?"

The doctor shrugged. "I can tell if the rope was consistent with the wounds. Do you have it?"

"In my desk drawer," Reese said.

"Bring it to me before I send the body to the undertaker." Doc Sterling sighed again and glanced up at the clock. "I guess you can bring Henry up, too."

"Is it my little girl?" Henry asked, jumping to his feet when Reese returned to his office.

Marshal Reese eased into the chair beside Henry Dale. "I'm sorry, Henry."

The man broke down, sobbing. "Oh, my God. My poor baby."

"I have the bastards who hurt her, Henry," Marshal Reese assured. "They'll pay for what they did to her."

Henry wiped his face with his sleeve. "What did they do to... to my baby, Marshal? Did she let them... the way that boy said in the saloon?"

"She didn't *let* them do anything, Henry," the Marshal snapped. "Those men tied her to a bed, beat, and abused your daughter. She wasn't in that shack because she wanted to be there. I promise you that." He patted Henry's shoulder. "I can take you to see her now."

Marshal Reese discreetly took the bloodstained ropes out of the drawer in his desk and tucked them into his waistband before escorting Henry Dale from the office.

8

Daisy woke when she heard noises coming from the kitchen below. When she heard the back door close, she pushed aside the quilt and lit the lamp beside the bed. She pulled the nightdress off over her head and then dressed in the same dress she'd worn the day before.

Carrying the glass lamp, Daisy crept down the narrow stairs to the kitchen. She suspected Carl had gone out to do the morning milking. From the bucket beside the sink, Daisy filled the coffee pot. She stoked the fire in the stove and added some wood.

By the time Carl returned with a bucket of fresh milk, Daisy had coffee boiling, biscuits in the oven, ham warmed, and eggs in the skillet.

"You didn't have to get up and make me breakfast, Daisy," he said, as he poured the milk into a large bowl to set in the icebox.

Daisy poured coffee and set the cups on the table. "The biscuits will be ready in a minute. How do you like your eggs?"

"Over easy, please," he said. "I've got a crock of cream waiting in the cellar. I just hate churning," he said with a chuckle as he took a seat and sipped his coffee.

"I can do that," Daisy said, as she turned the eggs. "Where do you keep your churn?"

Carl pointed to a shelf above the icebox. "Up there, but you don't have to do that."

Daisy smiled and brought two plates of eggs to the table along with golden-brown biscuits. "It's no bother, and that crock is close to empty," she said, nodding at the brown crock on the table.

"This is a right nice breakfast," he said, smiling at the pretty blonde, "and completely unexpected. Thank you."

"It's the least I could do," Daisy said as she sat. "You've been so kind with your hospitality."

They ate in nervous silence for a while. "I really shouldn't impose on you any longer, though," Daisy said. "Would it be too much of an imposition to ask you to drive me home? My mama and papa must be worried sick about me after all this time." She glanced down at the red welt on her exposed wrist and hastily pulled the cuff of the dress down to cover it.

Carl reached across the table and took the girl's trembling hand. "It's not an imposition at all, Daisy. I'm happy to do it." He emptied his coffee cup and got up to refill it. "I'm sure they'll be relieved to have you home."

Daisy scraped the last of the butter from the bottom of the crock and smeared it on her warm biscuit. "I hope you're right, Carl," she sighed. "My mama is a bit of a prude and might not understand what happened to me." Daisy tugged at the sleeve again.

"That's ridiculous," Carl chided. "What mama would blame her daughter for an ordeal like the one you went through?" He patted her hand reassuringly and then went on to finish his breakfast.

"I have to feed the hogs and gather the eggs from the chicken house," he said when he'd finished. "Then I'll hitch up the buggy, and we can go."

"Thank you, Carl," Daisy said. "I'll do up these dishes first."

Daisy trembled as they crossed Butte Creek and neared her parents' cabin.

"Your folks have fixed this place up a bit since I was here last," Carl said when the freshly painted house came into view.

Daisy rolled her eyes and smiled. "Mama insisted. She told Papa she wasn't gonna live in a rundown mining shack. She made him put in new doors and glass windows with shutters and flower boxes." Daisy smiled at the bright red geraniums she'd grown in the green boxes below the windows on the front of the small house.

"Looks nice," Carl said, pulling on the reins to stop the horses in front of the porch. "Want me to go in with you?" he asked when the girl didn't immediately jump down from the buggy and go rushing inside.

She turned with a weak smile on her bruised lips. "I thought they might come out when they heard the buggy."

"Maybe they're busy in the back and didn't hear."

Daisy snorted softly. "Not my mama. I swear she hears folks comin' as soon as they cross the creek back there."

Carl got down and helped Daisy from the buggy. He held her hand as they walked toward the neat porch. The voices of a man and woman drifted out through an open window, and Daisy pulled her hand from his as she stepped toward the door.

"You heard what people are saying that boy said in the saloon, Henry," they heard her mother say in a shrill voice. "He said she went with them willingly and then… and then begged them to do the things to her they did. She's as much a tramp as that Biggs girl."

"I don't think that's the case at all, Mama," they heard Henry say. "The Marshal said…"

"I don't care what the Marshal said, Henry," Lola snapped. "She probably spread her legs for him, too. She's always been a willful girl, and she's the reason I could never give you a son. She ruined my womb when she was being born." Lola took a deep breath. "She was willful even then. She ruined our chance to have a real family, and now she's ruined our reputation in this horrible community."

"Now, Lola," Henry sighed as they listened, "Paradice is a nice little town. It…"

"I'll never be able to hold my head up again!" Lola sobbed. "I want to go home, Henry. I want to go back to St. Louis, where nobody knows what a whore our daughter is. Please take me home and away from this shame."

Carl watched Daisy stiffen as she listened to her mother. He put a hand on her shoulder, but she flinched away from his touch. "Come on, Daisy," he whispered, "just go in. I'm sure they'll be glad to see you."

"No," she said and turned away from the door with tears streaming from her eyes. "I can't," she wept and walked back toward the wagon.

Carl followed with his mouth agape and helped Daisy back into the waiting buggy. "I'm sorry, Daisy," he said, but the girl put up her hand to silence him as she sobbed.

He turned the buggy around and rode away from the Dales' house without the arguing couple inside hearing a thing. Carl handed Daisy his blue kerchief when he heard her sniffing after the tears had finally stopped. She took it, wiped her face, and blew her nose.

"I'm sorry, Carl," she said after a while, as they bounced along the shady road back to his farm. "I don't know what I'm going to do now."

"You can stay with me for as long as you need to," he said, as the horse turned into the lane leading to the barn. "It gets lonely out here all alone."

"And you need someone to churn the butter," Daisy said with a nervous grin and wiped her face again.

Carl grinned back to reassure her. "That too."

"Won't people think it's improper, though?" Daisy asked.

"Nobody visits me out here since Mercy left with the children," he sighed, "and I have little reason to venture into town." He hesitantly took Daisy's hand from her lap. "You can stay here with me for as long as you want, Daisy. Ain't no one gonna know or judge either of us for it."

"That makes things simpler, I suppose. Thank you, Carl," Daisy said. She pulled her hand away and got down from the buggy. "I'll get to that churning then."

Carl watched the girl wearing one of Mercy's old dresses walk back toward the house. She hesitated at the pickets around the grave but walked on to the cellar and came up a few minutes later carrying the heavy crock of cream.

"It's nice havin' someone around to talk to," he said to the sweaty horse he'd unhitched from the buggy as he rubbed it down, smiling. "Someone who talks back from time to time."

9

"You two are under arrest for the rape and murder of Miss Daisy Dale," Marshal Reese said, after returning from the doctor's office where he'd left Henry weeping over his daughter's cold, battered body.

"*Rape?*" Jamison snorted indignantly. "We never raped nobody. That little bitch went up to the shack willingly and begged us to make a woman of her."

"You're a disgusting excuse for a human being, Jamison Earl," Marshal Reese hissed, "and I hope Judge Timmons sentences you to hang for what you did to that poor girl."

"Judge Timmons, huh?" Jamison said and winked at Jake in the other cell. "My daddy ain't gonna let his only son sit in jail for long, and he certainly ain't gonna let him hang for givin' a poke to some no-account little farm girl trash."

"I guess we'll see about that," the Marshal said and turned to leave.

"I demand to see my daddy, Marshal," Jamison yelled and kicked over the chamber pot, sending the smelly contents across the cell's hard-packed dirt floor.

Marshal Reese shook his head and grinned. "Like I told you and your *daddy* already, you can meet with your lawyer before Judge Timmons calls the hearing on your bail and not before."

46

"And when is the old coot supposed to be in Paradice?"

"A week or two," the Marshal said.

"You mean I gotta sit in this place for another week or two?" Jamison yelled and kicked the metal pot again before dropping back onto his bunk. "Then I guess you better clean this mess up."

"I didn't make it," the Marshal said before leaving the cell area and slamming the door.

Jamison stared across the cell at his friend. "Don't worry, Jake. My daddy will fix this. He's close friends with Timmons. I think he paid someone in Sacramento to have the bastard appointed to this circuit court in the first place."

"That's good, Jamison," Jake said, rubbing at his nose and fighting his queasy stomach to keep from gagging, "but did you have to kick over the shit can?"

Jamison snorted and stared at the door, the Marshal had closed. "That bastard will clean it up. It's his damned job."

Emmett Earl, dressed in his finest silk suit, sat in the Delta House sipping a glass of scotch as he waited for his guest to arrive.

"What is so important that it couldn't wait until I was in Paradice next week?" As he joined his old friend at the table in Sacramento's best restaurant, Judge Timmons asked.

"It's my boy, Marcus," Emmett said. "That damned Marshal in Paradice has arrested him for having relations with some silly little farm-girl and killing her."

"Did he?" the Judge asked and filled his glass with the amber liquid from the bottle on the table. "Kill her?"

"Of course not," Emmett protested. "My boy might be a little loose with the ladies, Marcus, but he's no killer, and those little tarts up there around Paradice fall down and spread their legs for him, hoping to trap him into a marriage with a baby in their belly."

Timmons nodded and sipped the fragrant scotch. "A problem for any young man from a prominent family. I'm surprised your boy isn't more careful with his seed."

Emmett chuckled. "Neither of us were when we were his age, as I recall."

"And look what it got us. I had to marry Pricilla Eddington, and you ended up with Doris Clark."

Emmett rolled his eyes. "Don't remind me. The woman is an absolute harpy and is after me night and day to get Jamison out of that damned jail." He pushed an envelope across the table to Timmons. "I'm hoping you can help me out with that."

The judge picked up the envelope, opened it discreetly, studied the contents, then tucked it into the inside pocket of his expensive jacket. "Tell Doris her boy will be home to sleep in his own bed very soon."

"I'm hoping we can forego an embarrassing trial as well," Emmett added, with a grin.

Judge Timmons frowned. "I can only go so far, Emmett. Let's see what sort of case the City Attorney puts forth at the arraignment next week. Tell your man Howl you want a bench trial rather than a jury. No need to rely on twelve other men to decide this when you can leave it to me."

"Thank you, Marcus," Emmett said, with a broad smile on his aging face. "I knew I could count on you." He stood and offered his hand to the judge. "Give Priscilla my regards."

"And Doris mine," the judge called, as he watched his friend walk away.

"We have to bury our girl, Lola," Henry implored. "She's been with the undertaker for three days."

"Nobody's going to come to the funeral of a whore, Henry."

Tired of listening to the lamentations of his wife, Henry stood. "Her papa will, and her mama should, too."

Lola glared up at the man towering over her with a stern look on his face. "You always spoiled her, Henry. It's no wonder she went bad."

"Our little girl did *not* go bad!" he stormed. "Those bastards grabbed her off the road and carried her up to that line shack. They beat her, Lola. I saw the bruises on her body." Tears wet his cheeks as he remembered his girl's swollen face as she lay on the doctor's table. "If you can't see yourself attending her funeral, Lola, then I think you should leave this house." He straightened and took a breath. "I'll give you the money to travel back to St. Louis."

"But I've got no one there anymore, Henry," Lola whimpered. "I want you to come back with me."

"Not until we see our girl in the ground," he said, "and those animals hung."

"Oh, Henry," she wailed, "you can't expect me to sit through a trial with everyone in town hearing what she let them do to her."

Henry grabbed his wife by the shoulders and shook her. "Our little girl didn't *let* any of this happen to her." He shoved his wife back into the chair. "I'm going to bury my baby." He took out his wallet, opened it, and pitched some bills at Lola. "That should be enough to book passage back to St. Louis. Be gone when I get back." Henry turned and stormed out of the house.

The funeral of the murdered girl was a sad affair. Her father showed up at the undertaker's, and they threw everything together in a rush. The girl had been laid out for days and had begun to smell. The flowers around her plain pine casket had done little to hide the stench.

The undertaker sent a runner to get the minister and the gravediggers.

Word spread quickly around Paradice, and soon people filled the pews in the small building. Women in black piled more flowers upon the closed casket and wept for the dead girl inside. Men stood at the back of the room, shaking their heads.

The minister said a few words in the stifling room and then called for prayer. The sun had risen high in the sky, warming the room. The girl's father gave tearful thanks to everyone for coming. Her mother arrived late, but everyone assumed that her grief had confined her to her bed.

The procession to the graveyard was like a sad holiday parade through Paradice. People who hadn't been at the undertaker's joined in along the way to the cemetery, and Judge Timmons got caught up in the procession on his way into town. Marshal Reese, and other men who'd been members of the search party, wept as they carried the casket on their shoulders and lowered it into the hastily dug grave.

The minister gave a moving graveside service, calling for a speedy and just trial for the heinous crime's perpetrators, and the crowd cheered. Judge Timmons stood nervously in the gathering, gauging their temperament. Finding Emmet's boy, innocent of the girl's murder, might not be as easy as he had initially thought. She'd been a true innocent and not some whoring doxie as Emmet had intimated in their meeting.

10

Carl enjoyed Daisy's company more than he could have imagined. She wasn't prettier than Mercy, but her disposition was like night and day compared with his wife's. Daisy found humor in the smallest thing and brought laughter back into the quiet house.

"What are your plans for today, Daisy?" he asked as she served breakfast. "I'm gonna start cutting hay in the field across the road."

"I'm gonna pick peaches," she said with a smile. "Looks like it will be a good harvest, and I want to get started canning so I can make you pies this winter."

"You're a good woman, Daisy," he said and reached for her hand.

Daisy pulled her hand away before he could touch it and began yanking at the cuffs of her sleeves to cover the red welts that persisted on her thin, pale wrists.

"I think you'd begin to heal, Daisy, if you could begin to forgive."

"Forgive?" she spat and sat, staring open-mouthed at the man across the table. "They hurt me, Carl, and they took everything from me. How am I supposed to forgive that?"

"I didn't say it would be easy," he said, brushing a hand nervously over a thin, red line across his throat, "but it makes the healing easier. Will you at least try?"

Daisy gave him a weak smile and reached for his hand. "I'll try," she whispered as she squeezed his warm, strong fingers. "As long as I'm here with you, I think I can. You give me a strength I never felt before."

Carl covered her hand with his other one and lifted it to his lips. He kissed it softly. "You've given me something too, Daisy," he said and smiled. "You've brought light back into my dark life."

Daisy blushed and turned away as her eyes filled with tears. "I wish I'd met you before--"

"We met at just the right time for the both of us," he said and kissed her hand again.

Unwilling to push his luck, Carl released her hand and stood. "That hay isn't gonna cut itself, so I'd best get after it." He patted her shoulder and fled through the back door.

Jamison sat with his father, Lawyer Howl, and Jake at the table in the center of the Marshal's cramped office.

"Howl," Emmett Earl said, as he glared at the two younger men, "will represent both of you in this matter, so I hope you have your stories straight."

"Oh yes, sir," Jake chirped, "we been practicin' it while we sat back there in our cells."

Jamison just sat grinning. "What was all that commotion we heard outside?" he asked, trying to loosen the starched collar of the new shirt his father had brought him to change into for the court hearing.

"The damned girl's funeral," Emmett snapped, shaking his gray head. "I think everyone in town turned out."

Jamison shrugged his shoulders and smirked. "Makes no never mind, Daddy, if the fix is in with Timmons like you said."

Emmett slapped his son's shoulder. "Will you watch your fool mouth, boy," he hissed as his eyes darted to the door and then to Howl, who swallowed hard. "Don't announce it to anyone who might be listening."

"Sorry, Daddy," Jamison said, rubbing his shoulder.

There was a knock at the door. It opened, and Marshal Reese poked his head inside. "Judge Timmons is ready," he said. "I'll walk with you up to the courthouse."

"I think we can walk to the damned courthouse without your help, Reese," Jamison snarled as he and the others stood.

"It's my job," the big Marshal said, as he held the door open.

With Lawyer Howl at his side, Emmett Earl led the group up the boardwalk with Jamison and Jake behind them, followed by Marshal Reese with a rifle in his hands.

Aware of the court proceedings, people lined the street and stood outside the brick courthouse. They hissed at the Earls and Jake Morgan as they passed, and some threw rotten vegetables and eggs.

"I hope you bastards hang for what you done to that poor girl!" someone yelled before an egg smashed into the side of Jamison's head and ran down his face.

"What the hell, Marshal?" Jamison growled and turned to glare at Reese, who handed him a clean kerchief to clean the stinking egg off his face.

"Still think you could have made it without an armed escort, asshole?" the Marshal said, with a satisfied grin.

"Jeez," Jamison groaned, "all we did was have a little fun with a worthless farm girl."

"Shut up," the Marshal hissed, cuffing the young man on the back of the head with the butt of his rifle, "or I'll give you to the *good* people of Paradice."

"Daddy!" Jamison howled as he stumbled forward.

Emmett Earl turned to glare at his only son. "Shut up, boy, and act like you have some dignity."

As they stepped into the crowded courthouse, Emmett brushed remnants of food from his expensive suit before joining his wife in a seat behind the defense table, where Howl, Jamison, and Jake took seats.

"All rise for the Honorable Marcus Timmons," someone called in a loud, clear voice, and everyone stood.

Marcus Timmons came from a door behind a tall desk, wearing a black robe, and took a seat. He stared out at the crowd with a stern look on his face. "You may be seated," he said, and everyone sat.

Jamison elbowed Jake and grinned. The grin faded, however, when he caught the scowl on Judge Timmons' face.

"How do the defendants plead?" he asked.

Lawyer Howl urged his clients to their feet. "These young men plead not guilty to these heinous accusations, Your Honor," Howl replied in a loud voice.

"Very well," the Judge said. "And what is the City Attorney's recommendation on bail?"

The City Attorney, a short, thin man who wore wire-rimmed spectacles on his beak-like nose, stood. "These two, Your Honor, are charged with the most heinous of crimes against an innocent young woman of this community. The City begs Your Honor to keep them incarcerated until their trial, for the safety and peace of mind of other young women and their parents."

"Oh, good lord," Jamison huffed and rolled his eyes. "She was a little tart who laid back and spread her legs for us the same as any other whore would."

The crowd erupted with hisses and slurs directed at Jamison Earl.

Judge Timmons pounded his gavel. "That will be enough of that, young man," the Judge chided. "Mr. Howl, please control your client in my courtroom."

"Yes, Your Honor," Howl said and glared at Jamison. "It won't happen again. My clients are reputable young men and will be under the supervision of Mr. Emmett Earl and his wife at their ranch some miles away from Paradice," Howl said confidently.

"Therefore, Your Honor, I ask that they be given bail, which Mr. Earl is more than able and willing to pay, or they are released on their own merits into the Earls' custody pending trial. We also request a speedy Bench Trial at Your Honor's earliest convenience."

The courtroom crowd went wild at the suggestion that the two might go free, and Judge Timmons began pounding his gavel. "Order!" he called in a loud, commanding voice. "I will have order in this court, or I'll have you all cleared out of here."

The uproar in the room subsided from yells to soft murmurs. Judge Timmons studied the scowling faces in his courtroom—all except

Jamison Earl, who sat with an irritating, smug grin on his young face. The Judge pounded the gavel again.

"I cannot in good conscience grant bail of any kind," he said and watched the grin fall from Jamison's face. "I fear for their safety here in Paradice and feel they will be safer confined in Marshal Reese's jail for the time being."

Reese smiled and nodded to the Judge while Jamison turned to stare at his wide-eyed father.

"I am, however," the Judge continued, "ready to hear this case now if both attorneys are ready to proceed."

Howl stood and smiled at his clients confidently. "The defense is ready to proceed, Your Honor."

"Mr. Cutter?" the Judge asked, looking to the City Attorney.

Cutter stood. "Without a doubt, Your Honor. The City of Paradice is ready to proceed in this matter.

Judge Timmons smiled. "Very well, as it is already after the noon hour, we will adjourn for today and meet back here at nine in the morning." He banged his gavel, stood, and left the courtroom.

Jamison turned to his parents. "What happened, Daddy? I thought you took care of this, and we'd be out of that damned jail today?"

With his wife's hand in his, Emmett glanced around at the scowling faces leaving the Court House. "Marcus was right, son," he said in a low voice. "This bunch would have cut us all down if he'd granted bail. They're like a pack of rabid coyotes and are out for blood—your blood if the walk from the jailhouse was any indication."

Doris Earl took her son's hand. "Don't worry, sweetheart," she sighed, "you'll be home tomorrow, and I'll have Martha make your favorite fried chicken supper and a big chocolate cake the way you like."

"Thank you, Mama," he said, then bent and kissed his mother's pale cheek.

Marshal Reese walked over with his rifle. "Take your time sayin' your goodbyes," he said. "I'm gonna give this bunch a chance to thin out before we head back to the jail for the night."

11
_____

B ecause it was a bench trial and no jury had to be empaneled,
spectators of the notorious trial filled the jury box, and the room
buzzed with excitement as Judge Timmons called the court to order.
Emmett and Doris Earl sat in the first row behind the defense table, and
Henry and Lola Dale sat in the row behind the City Attorney.

"Mr. Cutter," the Judge said, "you may call your first witness."

Cutter stood. "I call Mr. Paul Adams to the stand, Your Honor."

Paul stood, walked to the front, and swore to tell the truth.

"You're familiar with the defendants in this case?" Cutter asked.

"I am," Paul replied.

"And you happened to overhear Mr. Earl in the Pair O' Dice Saloon
on the night of Friday the ninth?"

"I did."

"And what was it you heard Mr. Earl say?" Cutter asked.

"He was tellin' me, Doug, and Brad that he and Jake had a girl up at a
line shack." He stopped, glancing nervously at Mr. and Mrs. Dale. "He
said they was havin' fun with her."

"What sort of fun, Mr. Adams? Please tell the court exactly what you
recall, Mr. Earl saying."

"But her folks are sittin' right there," Paul said to the Judge and nodded to the Dales.

"Mr. and Mrs. Dale," the Judge said, "Mr. Adams fears embarrassing you with this testimony. If you'd be more comfortable in the hall while he relates this testimony, you may leave, and we'll call you back when he's finished."

Henry bent and whispered with Lola before standing. "Thank you, Mr. Adams, for wanting to spare us, but we want to know what these animals did to our baby girl."

Howl jumped to his feet. "I object to the reference to my clients as animals, Your Honor."

Judge Timmons banged his gavel. "So, noted." He turned to Paul. "You may continue, young man. Please tell the court what you heard the defendant say on the night in question."

Paul stared at Henry. "Only if you're sure you want to hear this." Henry nodded, and Paul closed his eyes as he continued. "Jamison told us he had a pretty, blonde gal up at the line shack, and they'd been pokin' her in all her holes every day for a couple of weeks."

Gasps of shock issued from the crowd and Judge Timmons banged his gavel for quiet.

"Did Mr. Earl tell you the girl's name?" Cutter asked.

"No," Paul answered truthfully.

"Did he ever tell you where the girl came from... a whorehouse in Bridgeport, perhaps?"

"No, he said him, and Jake grabbed her up off the road and carried her up to the line shack. Jamison said he took her virginity in her cunny, and Jake took her ass, but he couldn't remember which of 'em took her in the mouth the first time."

Lola Dale gave a loud whimper and swooned into her husband's arms as others in the courtroom protested against Paul's graphic testimony, though most had already heard the rumors.

Judge Timmons pounded his gavel again. "If the salaciousness of the testimony, in this case, is going to be a problem, I will clear the room and hear the rest in private."

Henry Dale stood and turned to address the people in the room. "Please, folks," he pled. "Our daughter deserves justice. Hold your tongues so the testimony can be given and justice served." He returned to his seat and put an arm around his weeping wife.

"Thank you, Mr. Dale," Judge Timmons said, before turning back to Mr. Cutter. "Do you have more questions for this witness?"

"Only one or two," he said, and the Judge nodded. "What happened after Mr. Earl told you and your friends about this girl?"

Paul took a deep breath. "He said him and Jake had her tied up to a bed, so she'd still be there when they wanted to use her again, and he invited us up there so we could all have a taste."

"And did you all go?"

"No," Paul said, shaking his head. "Doug and Brad went with him, but I stayed behind and went to the Marshal with what I heard."

"Thank you, Mr. Adams," Cutter said. "Your witness, Mr. Howl."

Howl stood and stepped toward the witness box. "You don't like my defendant much, do you, Mr. Adams?"

"Which one?" Paul asked, glancing toward Jamison, who was grinning smugly, and Jake, who looked frightened and embarrassed.

"Mr. Earl," Howl said. "You don't like Mr. Earl much."

"No," Paul said. "He's a pig."

"Move to strike that comment from the record, Your Honor," Howl yelped.

"So, noted, Mr. Howl, but do you have anything probative of this witness?"

"I suppose not," Howl huffed. "Nothing further." He returned to his seat and dropped into it.

"Thank you, Mr. Adams," Judge Timmons said, "you're excused." He glanced up at Cutter. "Call your next witness, Mr. Cutter."

Cutter stood. "I call Marshal Ken Reese to the stand."

The Marshal strode to the front of the room, and the bailiff swore him in.

"Mr. Adams came to you with what he heard Mr. Earl say in the Pair O' Dice Saloon?" Cutter asked once the Marshal had taken his seat.

"He did," the Marshal answered in his deep, clear voice.

"And the two of you traveled up the mountain to the shack in question?"

"We did."

"And what did you find there when you arrived?"

Marshal Reese frowned. "Jamison Earl was there with two of his friends."

"And Miss Dale? Was she there?"

"No, she was not, but we heard Mr. Earl tell his friends that she'd been there, and he showed them the ropes they'd used to tie her to the bed."

Mrs. Dale gave a loud whimper, and the crowd began to murmur angrily. Judge Timmons pounded his gavel, and the courtroom settled.

Mr. Cutter picked up a handful of rope, carried it to the witness box, and handed it to Reese. "Are these the ropes, Marshal?"

The Marshal studied the lengths of coarse jute before returning them to Cutter. "They are."

"And how do you know that?" Cutter asked as he handed the ropes to the Judge.

"I recognize the blood," he said and turned to Judge Timmons. "They were still wet when I took them from the bed in the shack, and Jamison had just told his friends the girl had worn her wrists raw, trying to escape."

"Not something one would think a girl would do if she *wanted* to be sharing a bed with a young man," Cutter said, glaring at the defendants.

"Hardly," the Marshal replied firmly.

Howl jumped to his feet. "Calls for speculation, Your Honor. Does the City Attorney put forth that the Marshal knows what young women want when sharing a bed with a young man?"

"Only a nitwit would think a girl would *want* to be tied up and wear her wrists bloody," the Marshal chided, and the room broke out in tittering laughter.

Timmons chuckled as well and pounded his gavel to quiet the laughter. "He has a point, Mr. Howl, but I take your point as well. Mr. Cutter, please limit your questions to the witness's obvious expertise."

"Of course, Your Honor," the City Attorney said, with a grin tugging at his thin lips. "I'm sorry." He returned to the Marshal. "You were the one who found Miss Dale's body?"

"Me and Ray Curry," he said, "the next day."

"And she was in the general area of said line shack?"

"Less than a quarter of a mile away. Ray followed her tracks through the woods and down a steep hill to a branch of Butte Creek, where it looked like she'd curled up in a deer wallow to sleep—and then died."

"Thank you, Marshal." Cutter turned to Timmons. "I don't have any more questions for this witness."

Mr. Howl read over his notes before standing to question Reese. "What was the condition of the young woman's body, Marshal?"

Marshal Reese raised a thick brow. "She wasn't wearing any clothes, her wrists and ankles had rope burns, and it was obvious she'd suffered a severe beating over an extended period of time."

Howl ignored Mrs. Dale's sobs and went back to the table and read through his notes again. "You said you and Mr. Curry followed a trail through the trees, and it led down a steep hill."

"Yes."

"Could the young lady's injuries have occurred during a fall down said steep hill?"

Marshal Reese shrugged his broad shoulders and grinned. "Medicine not being my area of expertise, I suppose you'd have to ask the doc about such as that."

Howl frowned, realizing the Marshal hadn't fallen for his attempted guile. "Very well. I have no further questions for this witness."

"Thank you, Marshal," Judge Timmons said, "you're excused. Call your next witness, Mr. Cutter."

"The City calls Doctor Sterling to the stand."

The white-headed doctor stood and walked to the witness box. He gave his oath to tell the truth and then settled into the chair before the people in the courtroom.

"You examined the body of Miss Dale after the Marshal brought her in?" Cutter asked.

"I did." He scowled at Attorney Howl. "And she didn't get those bruises from rolling down no damned hill."

Curry smiled at the cranky old doctor. "How can you be certain of that, Doctor?"

"Young man," Doc Sterling snapped, "I've been a doctor for over thirty years. I've seen my share of injuries from saloon brawls in my day. That girl had fists used on her over a period of several days. Some of the bruises were yellow and near healed, while others were dark purple and fresh."

"And you determined the cause of death?" Curry persisted.

"She'd received a severe punch in the ribcage about here," the old doctor said, pointing to his upper left torso. "It broke a rib that punctured her lung, and she eventually drowned in her own blood."

Lola Dale sobbed from her seat.

"Is that all?" Cutter asked, after giving Mrs. Dale a chance to settle.

"Damn, boy," Doc Sterling hissed as he glanced at the girl's parents, "ain't that enough?"

"I'm sorry, Doctor, but the court must hear your complete findings concerning Miss Dale's condition when you examined her body."

"Very well," the doctor said. "The young woman had suffered severe trauma over the period of several days, resulting eventually in her death. I also found evidence of repeated sexual trauma. In my opinion, somebody forcibly abused Miss Dale also over a period of several days. She suffered deep ligature wounds on her wrists and ankles from a rope such as that which the Marshal delivered to me for comparison."

"How could you tell it was forced and not a consensual coupling, Doctor?"

Doc Sterling rolled his eyes and took a deep breath. "A woman's nether regions look a certain way after consensual coupling, and this young lady's did not look that way in the least," he admonished the attorney. "She suffered the kind of bruising and tearing I've only seen in cases of violent sexual assault while bound in place against her will."

"I see, Doctor," Cutter said. "Thank you." He turned to Howl. "Your witness, sir."

Howl stood. "Doctor," he said, "if a woman enjoyed sex on the rough side, would you expect to see her nether regions in that condition then?" He gave a slight giggle, but the crowd didn't find it amusing and remained silent.

The old doctor's eyes narrowed. "An experienced *woman* who has had the opportunity to experience life and know what she enjoyed, yes, but not an inexperienced girl who'd only just violently lost her virginity. The only way she'd have those kinds of injuries is from repeated forced penetration."

"In your expert opinion, Doctor," Howl asked, "could the young woman's death be attributed to her night out in the elements without any clothes?"

"Possibly," he said, "but it could be then lain directly at the feet of the ones who relieved her of those clothes." He glanced up at Judge Timmons. "Couldn't it?"

"I have no more questions for this witness," Howl snapped and dropped back into his seat at the defense table.

"Thank you, Doctor," Judge Timmons said, "You may step down. Your next witness, Mr. Cutter?"

The thin City Attorney stood. "The City rests, Your Honor."

Judge Timmons pounded his gavel. "We will break for a one hour lunch and then hear defense witnesses."

"Are you ready to proceed, Mr. Howl?" Timmons asked, once they'd returned from lunch and he'd called the court to order.

Howl stood with a nervous smile. "The defense calls Jamison Earl to the stand."

Jamison stood and strode cockily to the witness box. He was sworn in and took his seat.

Howl stepped forward. "You and Mr. Morgan have been charged with a very serious crime, Jamison…"

"Yeah, and it's all bullshit. We didn't rape that little tart," Jamison hissed. "We didn't have to force her to do anything. She wanted everything she got, and she liked it."

"She wanted to go to the shack with you and Mr. Morgan?"

Jamison smiled. "She sure did, sir. She was like all the greedy little cunnies in this town. She begged us to take her and make a woman of her." He grinned up at Judge Timmons.

"She probably thought she'd get a rich husband if she spread her legs and got a baby in her belly." He grinned out at the crowd. "It's what gals do. It's how my sister got a husband in the state senate in Sacramento and probably how my mama got my daddy, too."

There were gasps from women in the crowded courtroom, but he continued. "Hell, it's probably how the little bitch's mama got her daddy, too."

Lola Dale stood. "You're a foul-mouthed liar, young man. My

daughter wasn't like that. She was going to be a school teacher. She was a good girl. Too good for the likes of your sorta filth."

"Me and Jake taught her a thing or two, that's for certain," Jamison said with a chuckle.

"But you killed her!" Lola screamed. "Why did you have to kill her?" She fell into her husband's arms sobbing as Timmons pounded his gavel to restore order in his courtroom.

"I didn't kill the little bitch," Jamison spat and pointed at his co-defendant. "When I left, Jake had his cock in her tight little ass. If anybody killed the bitch it was him and not me."

"Did you see Mr. Morgan hit Miss Dale?" Howl asked. "Doctor Sterling has testified the injury to Miss Dale was the result of a punch to her ribs that punctured her lung."

"Sure," he said. "I saw him hit her lots of times." He grinned at his co-defendant. "As a matter of fact, I saw him punch her that very day after she bit his cock while he had it in her sweet little mouth."

Jake shot to his feet. "That's a lie, Jamison. You're the one who punched her because she bit your damned cock when you shoved it in her mouth."

"Someone had to teach her some manners. She shouldn't ought to have fought her betters and just given us what we wanted." He grinned at the Dales. "She'd likely be here today and not molderin' in that cemetery if she had. If you ask me, it's your fault for not teachin' your little bitch to have given it up to them who's better than her when they came for it, and you two should be the one's sittin' here on trial for her killin' and not poor Jake and me.

"You're an ass, Jamison," Jake spat before turning to the judge. "It was his idea to grab the girl off the road. She fought him, and he punched her in the face and knocked her out. He stripped her of her clothes and tied her to that bed. She begged him not to deflower her, but he wouldn't listen and took her with her screamin' and cryin' like a baby for her mama."

"You took her too, Jake," Jamison yelled from the witness stand. "Don't make out like I was the only one pokin' her sweet little holes and slappin' her around."

Jake turned to Henry and Lola. "He's right. I poked her, too, but I never hit her, and I untied her so she could use the chamber pot and gave her water when she asked. I even left her untied that night to give her arms a rest so she could sleep."

"And if you'd left the stupid little bitch tied up," Jamison hissed, "we wouldn't be in this mess right now."

The courtroom was a riot of angry voices, and the judge had given up pounding his gavel. He put his fingers to his mouth and let out a shrill whistle.

"Do you have anything further, Mr. Howl?"

"As the prosecution has not come close to making a case against my clients, Your Honor," Howl said confidently, "I call for a directed verdict of not guilty on all charges against my clients."

Timmons stared at the attorney with his mouth agape. "You can't be serious, Mr. Howl. Both of your clients as much as admitted their guilt in open court." The judge shot Emmett Earl an apologetic glance. "I have no choice but to render a verdict of guilty on all charges and will go directly to sentencing. Both defendants will be hung by the neck until dead at the earliest convenience of the marshal."

He pounded his gavel, stood to a cheering crowd, and left the courtroom.

12

Carl sat at the table, watching Daisy putting the finishing touches to supper. He'd kissed her for the first time that afternoon beneath the shade of the maples in the front yard. She hadn't flinched away, and she'd even kissed him back. It was more than he'd expected from the poor, damaged girl.

"Come sit with me, Daisy," Carl said and patted the empty chair beside him.

She turned to glance over her shoulder. "I need to put this pie in the oven first," she said and opened the oven. Daisy slid the pie inside, closed the oven door, and then went to the table. "What do you want to talk about?"

Carl took her hand. "I just thought we should talk."

"About?" she asked and pulled her hand away as she sat.

"I thought it might be obvious," he said. "What happened between us this afternoon."

Daisy averted her eyes and tugged at her sleeves. "I don't think I'm ready yet, Carl," she mumbled. "I appreciate your patience, but if you feel you must press me in this, I will go."

Carl reached for her hand again. "Don't go, Daisy," he pled. "I will attempt to be patient. I know they hurt you, and you need time to heal."

"I'm feeling better every day, Carl," she said, "but I'm not there yet. I enjoyed the kiss today, I really did, and I didn't know if I ever would after what happened to me."

"I know you are," he said and smiled. "I want you here, Daisy. This farm is the closest thing to Heaven I could ever imagine, and I want to share it with you. Mercy never felt that way about it, but I think you do."

"I appreciate that, and I do feel that way." She sighed and put a hand on his warm cheek as she stared around the spacious kitchen. "I'm trying, Carl. I really am."

He put his hand over hers and smiled. "I know you are, Daisy. I'll try to be patient."

Jamison cringed with every smack of the hammer as the carpenter constructed the gallows in the street outside the Paradice jail. "I can't believe this," he moaned, with his head in his hands. "She was just a two-bit farm tramp. How can they hang us over trash like her?"

"She was a human being like anyone else, and we killed her, Jamison. What we did to her was wrong, and we're gettin' what we deserve," Jake said, from the bunk in his cell.

"You may be," Jamison snorted, "but not me. I'm better than her any day and shouldn't be hangin' like a common criminal. It ain't right."

"I guess even your daddy couldn't buy you out of this mess, Jamison."

"We'll see about that," the arrogant young man said. "We ain't dead yet."

Jake rolled over and pulled the thin wool blanket over his head. "Not 'til mornin', anyway."

A hanging in Butte County, especially the hanging of a prominent citizen like Jamison Earl, was an event not to be missed. People from Paradice and across the county packed the main street to get a good spot to watch the two young men hang.

Henry and Lola Dale stood side-by-side, holding hands as Marshal Reese escorted the prisoners to the gallows. He had to urge Jamison Earl up the steep stairs, but Jake Morgan made his way up without putting up a fuss.

Emmett and Doris Earl sat in their buggy as the Marshal slipped the nooses around the necks of their son and his friend. Jamison scanned the crowd, and when he spotted them, he began to shout.

"You really gonna let them hang me, Daddy? She was just a two-bit farm tramp, Mama. She didn't count for nothin', and she loved every minute of—"

The floor dropping out from under him and the loud snap of his neck silenced Jamison Earl's rant. The people standing near the gallows watched the front of his trousers stain as his bladder released, and they smelled the stench as his bowels did the same.

The crowd stood silent for a minute, contemplating what they'd just witnessed, and then began to cheer. Mothers of young daughters could breathe easier, knowing they'd be safe from the likes of Jamison Earl and his friend Jake Morgan.

Emmett whipped his horse and took off for his ranch with Doris weeping bitterly beside him. Henry and Lola walked to the cemetery to give their daughter the news that justice had been served, in the hopes she'd rest easy now.

———

Daisy was sitting in one of the rocking chairs on the porch, snapping beans when she saw two riders coming across the field toward the house.

"Someone's coming, Carl," Daisy called into the house through the screen door.

The two cowboys stopped outside the fence and hopped from their horses. A chill ran down her spine when Daisy recognized the two men.

"Will you look who's sittin' there, Jake?" Jamison said as he opened the gate and strode into the yard. "I thought they said the little bitch was dead."

"Carl!" Daisy screamed, knocking the bowl of beans from her lap as she jumped to her feet.

"Where ya goin', sweetheart?" Jamison cooed as he strode toward the porch, stroking his crotch. "I think you owe me an' Jake a little somethin' for all the trouble you caused us."

Carl burst from the house with his shotgun in his hands. "What's goin' on out here, Daisy?"

"Now, who is this?" Jamison snarled but stopped when he saw the shotgun and the determination in the man's eyes as he swept Daisy behind him. "You pokin' this little bitch now, mister?"

"You fellas should best be on your way," Carl snapped, as he held Daisy, trembling, behind him. "You're not welcome here."

"They're the ones, Carl," Daisy whimpered into his back. "They're the men who hurt me up in that shack."

"Hurt you?" Jamison snorted as Jake stood by with an appalled look on his face. "It was the best you ever had, and you know it." He glanced up at Carl and grinned. "You should probably be thankin' Jake an' me for breakin' the little bitch in for ya, mister," Jamison said with a chuckle.

Carl swung the shotgun toward the offensive young man and pulled the trigger. Jamison grabbed at his midsection with his eyes wide in surprise. His lips moved, but no words came out as he crumpled to the ground.

Jake jumped away, waving his hands. "Don't shoot, mister. I just wanted to tell her how sorry I am for what happened."

Carl lowered his shotgun and took Daisy's trembling hand. "If that's true," he said, "then tell her, pick up that garbage, and be on your way."

"Yes, sir," Jake said, clearing his throat. "I'm sorry for what we done to ya, miss. It was wrong, and I hope ya can see it in your heart to forgive, though what we done was unforgivable."

Daisy took a tentative step forward, staring at the blood pooling around the body on the ground. "I'm tryin'," she said, tugging at her sleeves. "I'm tryin' to forgive, but it isn't easy."

Jake tipped his hat. "I can't ask for more." He bent and scooped Jamison's body up to carry back to his waiting horse.

"Are you all right?" Carl asked, putting an arm around Daisy's shoulders. "Some people don't deserve forgiveness," he said, as he watched Jake lead the horse away with Jamison's body draped over it.

She smiled up at him sheepishly. "I'm much better now," she whispered. She turned and put her arms around the handsome farmer. She pulled his head down to hers and kissed him. "And I think I'm ready for the next step." Daisy glanced at her wrists and smiled. For the first time in a long time, she didn't see the red welts marring her skin.

"Really?" he asked and pulled Daisy into his arms. "I've been waiting a long time to hear that." He kissed her again before carrying her into the house and his bedroom.

13

The two men sat on their horses, staring at the decaying farmhouse with dead trees surrounding it.

"It's a shame to see places like this falling into ruin," one of them said.

The other shook his head. "This is one of them places born in ruin. When I was a boy, my granddad used to tell me and my brother stories about this place on long winter nights."

"What kinda stories?" the younger man asked.

"You ain't never heard the stories about ol' Mercy Emmons?"

"The name sounds familiar, but no, I don't recall no stories." He took his hat off and wiped the sweat from his brow with his cotton shirt sleeve. "Who was she, and what did she do?"

The old man took a deep breath after taking a sip of water from his canteen. "That there," he said, pointing to the old farmhouse, "was the Emmons' place. Carl Emmons and his wife Mercy lived there with their four youngins. On Christmas Eve one year, Mercy went batshit crazy and cut all their throats while they slept."

"Jesus Christ," the younger man whistled. "Why the hell would she do a thing like that?"

The old man shook his head and shrugged. "No one ever knew. My granddaddy was one of the fellas who found her body a few days later. It was one of them winters when we had a warm spell, and it had been rainin'. Butte Creek over there," he said, pointing to the west, "had overflowed its banks a good bit. They found her in her bloody nightdress, froze half in and half out of the water with the damned knife still in her hand."

The younger cowboy shook his head. "Ain't that about where you found the body of that Dale gal some years back?"

"Sure is," the old man sighed. "Me an' ol' Marshal Reese was the ones who found that one."

"I'm surprised she didn't light out for this place," the younger man said, staring at the farmhouse.

"That place hadn't been lived in for close to forty years by the time that poor gal died," the old man said. "After one of the Emmons' hands came to work, heard the baby cryin', and came in and found all the rest dead in their beds, the place was abandoned."

"Abandoned?" the young cowboy said, shaking his head. "A nice place like this?" Something brought him back to the old man's story. "What, baby? I thought you said she killed them all."

"All but the baby in his cradle." The old man sighed as he stared across the field. "You know what's really spooky about this story?"

"No, what?"

The old man pointed to the house. "His hands buried Carl in a plot in the back yard," he said, "but Mercy's mama and daddy took her and the dead children to their ranch and buried them there."

"So?"

"They took the baby, too. They changed his name from Emmett Emmons to Emmett Earl and raised him as their son—not their grandson."

The younger man's eyes went wide. "You mean...?"

"Yep," the old man said. "The boy they hanged for killin' that Dale girl was ol' Carl Emmons' grandson."

"Oh, my lord," the younger cowboy whistled. "Now, that *is* spooky." He peered across the valley. "So, this is on Earl's property?"

"Yep," the old cowboy sighed, "the southeast corner of the ranch. Ol' man Earl deeded it to Emmons when he married his daughter, Mercy."

71

He pointed to the farm. "Used to be a right nice farm, too. There were peach trees out back by the barn. Me an' my little brother used to sneak over here and fill sacks with 'em for our mama when they got ripe, but a big storm blew down the barn back in '94 and took out the trees when it fell."

"That's a shame," the young cowboy said. "What ya think is gonna happen to it now that old Doris is dead?"

"Our way of life is dyin', boy," the old cowboy said. "When this war in Europe is over, I hear tell Teddy's bunch in Washington are gonna turn the whole west into one big National Park."

The younger man snorted as they turned their mounts back toward Paradice. "I'm gonna do like ol' Butch Cassidy and move to South America."

"Fat lotta good it did 'em," the old man said with a chuckle as they rode away.

"Who do you think they were?" As she and Carl stood on the porch, Daisy asked, leaning against one of the white posts.

Carl shrugged as he put an arm around Daisy. "I've got no idea. We used to get lots of company out here, but since Mercy left with the children, folks just don't come around like they once did."

Daisy kissed his cheek. "We have one another, Carl, and that's really all we need here in our little piece of Heaven. Isn't it?"

Carl took her into his strong arms and smiled. "It certainly is, Daisy." He bent and kissed her sweet, warm lips. "I've never been happier."

"Me too. Now, let's have some pie. The peach crop was good this year. I hope you don't get tired of eating them."

Dear reader,

We hope you enjoyed reading *A Tale For A Long Winter's Night*. Please take a moment to leave a review, even if it's a short one. Your opinion is important to us.

Discover more books by Lori Beasley Bradley at

https://www.nextchapter.pub/authors/lori-beasley-bradley

Want to know when one of our books is free or discounted? Join the newsletter at

http://eepurl.com/bqqB3H

Best regards,

Lori Beasley Bradley and the Next Chapter Team

Lightning Source UK Ltd.
Milton Keynes UK
UKHW010627210121
377450UK00001B/187